PENGUIN BOOKS

Six Feet of the Country

Nadine Gordimer was born and lives in South Africa. She has written eight collections of short stories and eight novels, of which *The Soft Voice of the Serpent*, *A World of Strangers*, *A Guest of Honour*, *Livingstone's Companions*, *The Conservationist*, *The Late Bourgeois World*, *Burger's Daughter*, *July's People*, *A Soldier's Embrace*, *Selected Stories* and *Something Out There* have been published in Penguin. This volume contains stories from both *A Soldier's Embrace* and *Selected Stories*. Among the literary prizes she has received are the Booker Prize and the French international award, the Grand Aigle d'Or. She was awarded the Scottish Arts Council's Neil Gunn Fellowship for 1981.

NADINE GORDIMER

Six Feet of the Country

PENGUIN BOOKS

Penguin Books Ltd, Harmondsworth, Middlesex, England
Viking Penguin Inc., 40 West 23rd Street, New York, New York 10010, U.S.A.
Penguin Books Australia Ltd, Ringwood, Victoria, Australia
Penguin Books Canada Limited, 2801 John Street, Markham, Ontario, Canada L3R 1B4
Penguin Books (N.Z.) Ltd, 182–190 Wairau Road, Auckland 10, New Zealand

In Great Britain: 'Six Feet of the Country' was first published in the volume *Six Feet in the Country*, Victor Gollancz Ltd, 1956; 'Good Climate, Friendly Inhabitants', 'A Chip of Glass Ruby' and 'Not For Publication' were first published in the volume *Not For Publication*, Victor Gollancz Ltd, 1965; 'City Lovers' (first published as 'Town and Country Lovers: *One*'), 'Country Lovers' (first published as 'Town and Country Lovers: *Two*') and 'Oral History' were first published in *Harper's and Queen*.

In the United States of America: 'Good Climate, Friendly Inhabitants' appeared originally in *Harper's* under the title 'Stranger in Town' and was first published in the volume *Not for Publication* (The Viking Press, Inc., 1965). 'A Chip of Glass Ruby' appeared originally in the *Atlantic Monthly* and was first published in the volume *Not for Publication*. 'City Lovers' and 'Country Lovers' appeared originally in the *New Yorker* under the title 'City Lovers' and were first published in the volume *A Soldier's Embrace* (The Viking Press, 1980) under the title 'Town and Country Lovers'. 'Not for Publication' appeared originally in the *Atlantic Monthly* under the title 'Praise' and was first published in the volume *Not for Publication*. 'Oral History' appeared originally in *Playboy* and was first published in the volume *A Soldier's Embrace*.

This selection first published in Great Britain 1982
Reprinted 1982, 1984, 1985, 1986

This selection first published in the United States of America 1986

Set in Linotron Baskerville by
Rowland Phototypesetting Ltd,
Bury St Edmunds, Suffolk
Printed and bound in Great Britain by
Cox & Wyman Ltd, Reading

Contents

Six Feet of the Country

My wife and I are not real farmers – not even Lerice, really. We bought our place, ten miles out of Johannesburg on one of the main roads, to change something in ourselves, I suppose; you seem to rattle about so much within a marriage like ours. You long to hear nothing but a deep satisfying silence when you sound a marriage. The farm hasn't managed that for us, of course, but it has done other things, unexpected, illogical. Lerice, who I thought would retire there in Chekhovian sadness for a month or two, and then leave the place to the servants while she tried yet again to get a part she wanted and become the actress she would like to be, has sunk into the business of running the farm with all the serious intensity with which she once imbued the shadows in a playwright's mind. I should have given it up long ago if it had not been for her. Her hands, once small and plain and well kept – she was not the sort of actress who wears red paint and diamond rings – are hard as a dog's pads.

I, of course, am there only in the evenings and at weekends. I am a partner in a travel agency which is flourishing – needs to be, as I tell Lerice, in order to carry the farm. Still, though I know we can't afford it, and though the sweetish smell of the fowls Lerice breeds sickens me, so that I avoid going past their runs, the farm is beautiful in a way I had almost forgotten – especially on a Sunday morning when I get up and go out into the paddock and see not the palm trees and fishpond and imitation-stone bird bath of the suburbs but white ducks on the dam, the lucerne field brilliant as window-dresser's grass, and the little, stocky, mean-eyed bull, lustful but bored, having his face tenderly licked by one of his ladies. Lerice comes out with her hair uncombed, in her hand a stick dripping with cattle dip. She will stand and look dreamily for a moment, the way she would pretend to look sometimes in those plays. 'They'll mate tomorrow,' she will say. 'This is their second day. Look how she loves him, my little Napoleon.' So that when people come to see us on Sunday afternoon, I am likely to hear myself saying as I pour out the drinks, 'When I drive back home from the city every day past those rows of suburban houses, I wonder how the devil we ever did stand it . . . Would you care to look around?' And there I am, taking some pretty girl and her husband stumbling down to our riverbank, the girl catching her stockings on the mealie-stooks and stepping over cow turds humming with jewel-green flies while she says, '. . . the *tensions* of the damned city. And you're near enough to get into town to a show, too! I think it's wonderful. Why, you've got it both ways!'

And for a moment I accept the triumph as if I *had* managed it – the impossibility that I've been trying for all my life: just as if the truth was that you could get it 'both ways', instead of finding yourself with not even one way or the other but a third, one you had not provided for at all.

But even in our saner moments, when I find Lerice's earthy enthusiasms just as irritating as I once found her histrionical ones, and she finds what she calls my 'jealousy' of her capacity for enthusiasm as big a proof of my inadequacy for her as a mate as ever it was, we do believe that we have at least honestly escaped those tensions peculiar to the city about which our visitors speak. When Johannesburg people speak of 'tension', they don't mean hurrying people in crowded streets, the struggle for money, or the general competitive character of city life. They mean the guns under the white men's pillows and the burglar bars on the white men's windows. They mean those strange moments on city pavements when a black man won't stand aside for a white man.

Out in the country, even ten miles out, life is better than that. In the country, there is a lingering remnant of the pre-transitional stage; our relationship with the blacks is almost feudal. Wrong, I suppose, obsolete, but more comfortable all around. We have no burglar bars, no guns. Lerice's farm boys have their wives and their piccanins living with them on the land. They brew their sour beer without the fear of police raids. In fact, we've always rather prided ourselves that the poor devils have nothing much to fear, being with us; Lerice even keeps an eye on their children, with all the competence of a woman who has never had a child of her own, and she certainly doctors them all – children and adults – like babies whenever they happen to be sick.

It was because of this that we were not particularly startled one night last winter when the boy Albert came knocking at our window long after we had gone to bed. I wasn't in our bed but sleeping in the little dressing-room-cum-linen-room next door, because Lerice had annoyed me and I didn't want to find myself softening towards her simply because of the sweet smell of the talcum powder on her flesh after her bath. She came and woke me up. 'Albert says one of the boys is very sick,' she said. 'I think you'd better go down and see. He wouldn't get us up at this hour for nothing.'

'What time is it?'

'What does it matter?' Lerice is maddeningly logical.

I got up awkwardly as she watched me – how is it I always feel a fool when I have deserted her bed? After all, I know from the way she never looks at me when she talks to me at breakfast next day that she is hurt and humiliated at my not wanting her – and I went out, clumsy with sleep.

'Which of the boys is it?' I asked Albert as we followed the dance of my torch.

'He's too sick. Very sick,' he said.

'But who? Franz?' I remembered Franz had had a bad cough for the past week.

Albert did not answer; he had given me the path, and was walking along beside me in the tall dead grass. When the light of the torch caught his face, I saw that he looked acutely embarrassed. 'What's this all about?' I said.

He lowered his head under the glance of the light. 'It's not me, baas. I don't know. Petrus he send me.'

Irritated, I hurried him along to the huts. And there, on Petrus's iron bedstead, with its brick stilts, was a young man, dead. On his forehead there was still a light, cold sweat; his body was warm. The boys stood around as they do in the kitchen when it is discovered that someone has broken a dish – uncooperative, silent. Somebody's wife hung about in the shadows, her hands wrung together under her apron.

I had not seen a dead man since the war. This was very different. I felt like the others – extraneous, useless. 'What was the matter?' I asked.

The woman patted at her chest and shook her head to indicate the painful impossibility of breathing.

He must have died of pneumonia.

I turned to Petrus. 'Who was this boy? What was he doing here?' The light of a candle on the floor showed that Petrus was weeping. He followed me out the door.

When we were outside, in the dark, I waited for him to speak. But he didn't. 'Now, come on, Petrus, you must tell me who this boy was. Was he a friend of yours?'

'He's my brother, baas. He came from Rhodesia to look for work.'

The story startled Lerice and me a little. The young boy had walked down from Rhodesia to look for work in Johannesburg, had caught a chill from sleeping out along the way and had lain ill in his brother Petrus's hut since his arrival three days before. Our boys had been frightened to ask us for help for him because we had never been intended ever to know of his presence. Rhodesian natives are barred from entering the Union unless they have a permit; the young man was an illegal immigrant. No doubt our boys had managed the whole thing successfully several times before; a number of relatives must have walked the seven or eight hundred miles from poverty to the paradise of zoot suits, police raids and black slum townships that is their *Egoli*, City of Gold – the African name for Johannesburg. It was merely a matter of getting such a man to lie low on our farm until a job could be found with someone who would be glad to take the risk of prosecution for employing an illegal immigrant in exchange for the services of someone as yet untainted by the city.

Well, this was one who would never get up again.

'You would think they would have felt they could tell *us*,' said Lerice next morning. 'Once the man was ill. You would have thought at least –' When she is getting intense over something, she has a way of standing in the middle of a room as people do when they are shortly to leave on a journey, looking searchingly about her at the most familiar objects as if she had never seen them before. I had noticed that in Petrus's presence in the kitchen, earlier, she had had the air of being almost offended with him, almost hurt.

In any case, I really haven't the time or inclination any more to go into everything in our life that I know Lerice, from those alarmed and pressing eyes of hers, would like us to go into. She is the kind of woman who doesn't mind if she looks plain, or odd; I don't suppose she would even care if she knew how strange she looks when her whole face is out of proportion with urgent uncertainty. I said, 'Now I'm the one who'll have to do all the dirty work, I suppose.'

She was still staring at me, trying me out with those eyes – wasting her time, if she only knew.

'I'll have to notify the health authorities,' I said calmly. 'They can't just cart him off and bury him. After all, we don't really know what he died of.'

She simply stood there, as if she had given up – simply ceased to see me at all.

I don't know when I've been so irritated. 'It might have been something contagious,' I said. 'God knows.' There was no answer.

I am not enamoured of holding conversations with myself. I went out to shout to one of the boys to open the garage and get the car ready for my morning drive to town.

As I had expected, it turned out to be quite a business. I had to notify the police as well as the health authorities, and answer a lot of tedious questions: How was it I was ignorant of the boy's presence? If I did not supervise my native quarters, how did I know that that sort of thing didn't go on all the time? And when I flared up and told them that so long as my natives did their work, I didn't think it my right or concern to poke my nose into their private lives, I got from the coarse, dull-witted police sergeant one of those looks that come not from any thinking process going on in the brain but from that faculty common to all who are possessed by the master-race theory – a look of insanely inane certainty. He grinned at me with a mixture of scorn and delight at my stupidity.

Then I had to explain to Petrus why the health authorities had to take away the body for a post-mortem – and, in fact, what a post-mortem was. When I telephoned the health department some days later to find out the result, I was told that the cause of death was, as we had thought, pneumonia, and that the body had been suitably disposed of. I went out to where Petrus was mixing a mash for the fowls and told him that it was all right, there would be no trouble; his brother had died from that pain in his chest. Petrus put down the paraffin tin and said, 'When can we go to fetch him, baas?'

'To fetch him?'

'Will the baas please ask them when we must come?'

I went back inside and called Lerice, all over the house. She came down the stairs from the spare bedrooms, and I said, '*Now* what am I going to do? When I told Petrus, he just asked calmly when they could go and fetch the body. They think they're going to bury him themselves.'

'Well, go back and tell him,' said Lerice. 'You must tell him. Why didn't you tell him then?'

When I found Petrus again, he looked up politely. 'Look, Petrus,' I said. 'You can't go to fetch your brother. They've done it already – they've *buried* him, you understand?'

'Where?' he said slowly, dully, as if he thought that perhaps he was getting this wrong.

'You see, he was a stranger. They knew he wasn't from here, and they didn't know he had some of his people here so they thought they must bury him.' It was difficult to make a pauper's grave sound like a privilege.

'Please, baas, the baas must ask them.' But he did not mean that he wanted to know the burial place. He simply ignored the incomprehensible machinery I told him had set to work on his dead brother; he wanted the brother back.

'But, Petrus,' I said, 'how can I? Your brother is buried already. I can't ask them now.'

'Oh, baas!' he said. He stood with his bran-smeared hands uncurled at his sides, one corner of his mouth twitching.

'Good God, Petrus, they won't listen to me! They can't, anyway. I'm sorry, but I can't do it. You understand?'

He just kept on looking at me, out of his knowledge that white men have everything, can do anything; if they don't, it is because they won't.

And then, at dinner, Lerice started. 'You could at least phone,' she said.

'Christ, what d'you think I am? Am I supposed to bring the dead back to life?'

But I could not exaggerate my way out of this ridiculous responsibility that had been thrust on me. 'Phone them up,' she went on. 'And at least you'll be able to tell him you've done it and they've explained that it's impossible.'

She disappeared somewhere into the kitchen quarters after coffee. A little later she came back to tell me, 'The old father's coming down from Rhodesia to be at the funeral. He's got a permit and he's already on his way.'

Unfortunately, it was not impossible to get the body back. The authorities said that it was somewhat irregular, but that since the hygiene conditions had been fulfilled, they could not refuse permission for exhumation. I found out that, with the undertaker's charges, it would cost twenty pounds. Ah, I thought, that settles it. On five pounds a month, Petrus won't have twenty pounds – and just as well, since it couldn't do the dead any good. Certainly I should not offer it to him myself. Twenty pounds – or anything else within reason, for that matter – I would have spent without grudging it on doctors or medicines that might have helped the boy when he was alive. Once he was dead, I had no intention of encouraging Petrus to throw away, on a gesture, more than he spent to clothe his whole family in a year.

When I told him, in the kitchen that night, he said, 'Twenty pounds?'

I said, 'Yes, that's right, twenty pounds.'

For a moment, I had the feeling, from the look on his face, that he was calculating. But when he spoke again I thought I must have imagined it. 'We must pay twenty pounds!' he said in the faraway voice in which a person speaks of something so unattainable it does not bear thinking about.

'All right, Petrus,' I said, and went back to the living room.

The next morning before I went to town, Petrus asked to see me. 'Please, baas,' he said, awkwardly, handing me a bundle of notes. They're so seldom on the giving rather than the receiving side, poor devils, they don't really know how to hand money to a white man. There it was, the twenty pounds, in ones and halves, some creased and folded until they were soft as dirty rags, others smooth and fairly new – Franz's money, I suppose, and Albert's, and Dora the cook's, and Jacob the gardener's, and God knows who else's besides, from all the farms and small holdings round about. I took it in irritation more than in astonishment, really – irritation at the waste, the uselessness of this sacrifice by people so poor. Just like the poor everywhere, I thought, who stint themselves the decencies of life in order to ensure themselves the decencies of death. So incomprehensible to people like Lerice and me, who regard life as something to be spent extravagantly and, if we think about death at all, regard it as the final bankruptcy.

The farm hands don't work on Saturday afternoon anyway, so it was a good day for the funeral. Petrus and his father had borrowed our donkey-cart to fetch the coffin from the city, where, Petrus told Lerice on their return, everything was 'nice' – the coffin waiting for them, already sealed up to save them from what must have been a rather unpleasant sight after two weeks' interment. (It had taken all that time for the authorities and the undertaker to make the final arrangements for moving the body.) All morning, the coffin lay in Petrus's hut, awaiting the trip to the little old burial ground, just outside the eastern boundary of our farm, that was a relic of the days when this was a real farming district rather than a fashionable rural estate. It was pure chance that I happened to be down there near the fence when the procession came past; once again Lerice had forgotten her promise to me and had made the house uninhabitable on a Saturday afternoon. I had come home and been infuriated to find her in a pair of filthy old slacks and with her hair uncombed since the night before, having all the varnish scraped from the living-room floor, if you please. So I had taken my No. 8 iron and gone off to practise my approach shots. In my annoyance, I had forgotten about the funeral, and was reminded only when I saw the procession coming up the path along the outside of the fence towards me; from where I was standing, you can see the graves quite clearly, and that day the sun glinted on bits of broken pottery, a lopsided homemade cross, and jam-jars brown with rain-water and dead flowers.

I felt a little awkward, and did not know whether to go on hitting my golf ball or stop at least until the whole gathering was decently past. The donkey-cart creaks and screeches with every revolution of the wheels, and it came along in a slow, halting fashion somehow peculiarly suited to the two donkeys who drew it, their little potbellies rubbed and rough, their heads sunk between the shafts, and their ears flattened back with an air submissive and downcast; peculiarly suited, too, to the group of men and women who came along slowly behind. The patient ass. Watching, I thought, you can see now why the creature became a Biblical symbol. Then the procession drew level with me and stopped, so I had to put down my club. The coffin was taken down off the cart – it was a shiny, yellow-varnished wood, like cheap furniture – and the donkeys twitched their ears against the flies. Petrus, Franz, Albert and the old father from Rhodesia hoisted it on their shoulders and the procession moved on, on foot. It was really a very awkward moment. I stood there rather foolishly at the fence, quite still, and slowly they filed past, not looking up, the four men bent beneath the shiny wooden box, and the straggling troop of mourners. All of them were servants or neighbours' servants whom I knew as casual easygoing gossipers about our lands or kitchen. I heard the old man's breathing.

I had just bent to pick up my club again when there was a sort of jar in the flowing solemnity of their processional mood; I felt it at once, like a wave of heat along the air, or one of those sudden currents of cold catching at your legs in a placid stream. The old man's voice was muttering something; the people had stopped, confused, and they bumped into one another, some pressing to go on, others hissing them to be still. I could see that they were embarrassed, but they could not ignore the voice; it was much the way that the mumblings of a prophet, though not clear at first, arrest the mind. The corner of the coffin the old man carried was sagging at an angle; he seemed to be trying to get out from under the weight of it. Now Petrus expostulated with him.

The little boy who had been left to watch the donkeys dropped the reins and ran to see. I don't know why – unless it was for the same reason people crowd around someone who has fainted in a cinema – but I parted the wires of the fence and went through, after him.

Petrus lifted his eyes to me – to anybody – with distress and horror. The old man from Rhodesia had let go of the coffin entirely, and the three others, unable to support it on their own, had laid it on the ground, in the pathway. Already there was a film of dust lightly wavering up its shiny sides. I did not understand what the old man was saying; I hesitated to interfere. But now the whole seething group turned on my silence. The old man himself came over to me, with his hands outspread and shaking, and spoke directly to me, saying something that I could tell from the tone, without understanding the words, was shocking and extraordinary.

'What is it, Petrus? What's wrong?' I appealed.

Petrus threw up his hands, bowed his head in a series of hysterical shakes, then thrust his face up at me suddenly. 'He says, "My son was not so heavy." '

Silence. I could hear the old man breathing; he kept his mouth a little open, as old people do.

'My son was young and thin,' he said at last, in English.

Again silence. Then babble broke out. The old man thundered against everybody; his teeth were yellowed and few, and he had one of those fine, grizzled, sweeping moustaches one doesn't often see nowadays, which must have been grown in emulation of early Empire-builders. It seemed to frame all his utterances with a special validity. He shocked the assembly; they thought he was mad, but they had to listen to him. With his own hands he began to prise the lid off the coffin and three of the men came forward to help him. Then he sat down on the ground; very old, very weak and unable to speak, he merely lifted a trembling hand towards what was there. He abdicated, he handed it over to them; he was no good any more.

They crowded round to look (and so did I), and now they forgot the nature of this surprise and the occasion of grief to which it belonged, and for a few minutes were carried up in the astonishment of the surprise itself. They gasped and flared noisily with excitement. I even noticed the little boy who had held the donkeys jumping up and down, almost weeping with rage because the backs of the grownups crowded him out of his view.

In the coffin was someone no one had seen before: a heavily built, rather light-skinned native with a neatly stitched scar on his forehead – perhaps from a blow in a brawl that had also dealt him some other, slower-working injury that had killed him.

I wrangled with the authorities for a week over that body. I had the feeling that they were shocked, in a laconic fashion, by their own mistake, but that in the confusion of their anonymous dead they were helpless to put it right. They said to me, 'We are trying to find out,' and 'We are still making inquiries.' It was as if at any moment they might conduct me into their mortuary and say, 'There! Lift up the sheets; look for him – your poultry boy's brother. There are so many black faces – surely one will do?'

And every evening when I got home, Petrus was waiting in the kitchen. 'Well, they're trying. They're still looking. The baas is seeing to it for you, Petrus,' I would tell him. 'God, half the time I should be in the office I'm driving around the back end of town chasing after this affair,' I added aside, to Lerice, one night.

She and Petrus both kept their eyes turned on me as I spoke, and, oddly, for those moments they looked exactly alike, though it sounds impossible: my wife, with her high, white forehead and her attenuated Englishwoman's body, and the poultry boy, with his horny bare feet below khaki trousers tied at the knee with string and the peculiar rankness of his nervous sweat coming from his skin.

'What makes you so indignant, so determined about this now?' said Lerice suddenly.

I stared at her. 'It's a matter of principle. Why should they get away with a swindle? It's time these officials had a jolt from someone who'll bother to take the trouble.'

She said, 'Oh.' And as Petrus slowly opened the kitchen door to leave, sensing that the talk had gone beyond him, she turned away, too.

I continued to pass on assurances to Petrus every evening, but although what I said was the same and the voice in which I said it was the same, every evening it sounded weaker. At last, it became clear that we would never get Petrus's brother back, because nobody really knew where he was. Somewhere in a graveyard as uniform as a housing scheme, somewhere under a number that didn't belong to him, or in the medical school, perhaps, laboriously reduced to layers of muscle and strings of nerve? Goodness knows. He had no identity in this world anyway.

It was only then, and in a voice of shame, that Petrus asked me to try and get the money back.

'From the way he asks, you'd think he was robbing his dead brother,' I said to Lerice later. But as I've said, Lerice had got so intense about this business that she couldn't even appreciate a little ironic smile.

I tried to get the money; Lerice tried. We both telephoned and wrote and argued, but nothing came of it. It appeared that the main expense had been the undertaker, and after all he had done his job. So the whole thing was a complete waste, even more of a waste for the poor devils than I had thought it would be.

The old man from Rhodesia was about Lerice's father's size, so she gave him one of her father's old suits, and he went back home rather better off, for the winter, than he had come.

Good Climate, Friendly Inhabitants

In the office at the garage eight hours a day I wear mauve linen overalls – those snappy uniforms they make for girls who aren't really nurses. I'm forty-nine but I could be twenty-five except for my face and my legs. I've got that very fair skin and my legs have gone mottled, like Roquefort cheese. My hair used to look pretty as chickens' fluff, but now it's been bleached and permed too many times. I wouldn't admit this to anyone else, but to myself I admit everything. Perhaps I'll get one of those wigs everyone's wearing. You don't have to be short of hair, any more, to wear a wig.

I've been years at the garage – service station, as it's been called since it was rebuilt all steel and glass. That's at the front, where the petrol pumps are; you still can't go into the workshop without getting grease on your things. But I don't have much call to go there. Between doing the books you'll see me hanging about in front for a breath of air, smoking a cigarette and keeping an eye on the boys. Not the mechanics – they're all white chaps of course (bunch of ducktails they are, too, most of them) – but the petrol attendants. One boy's been with the firm twenty-three years – sometimes you'd think he owns the place; gets my goat. On the whole they're not a bad lot of natives, though you get a cheeky bastard now and then, or a thief, but he doesn't last long, with us.

We're just off the Greensleeves suburban shopping centre with the terrace restaurant and the fountain, and you get a very nice class of person coming up and down. I'm quite friends with some of the people from the luxury flats round about; they wouldn't pass without a word to me when they're walking their dogs or going to the shops. And of course you get to know a lot of the regular petrol customers, too. We've got two Rolls and any amount of sports cars who never go anywhere else. And I only have to walk down the block to Maison Claude when I get my hair done, or in to Mr Levine at the Greensleeves Pharmacy if I feel a cold coming on.

I've got a flat in one of the old buildings that are still left, back in town. Not too grand, but for ten quid a month and right on the bus route . . . I was married once and I've got a lovely kid – married since she was seventeen and living in Rhodesia; I couldn't stop her. She's very happy with him and they've got twin boys, real little toughies! I've seen them once.

There's a woman friend I go to the early flicks with every Friday, and the Versfelds' where I have a standing invitation for Sunday lunch. I think they depend on me, poor old things; they never see anybody. That's the trouble when you work alone in an office, like I do, you don't make friends at your work. Nobody to talk to but those duckies in the workshop, and what can I have in common with a lot of louts in black leather jackets? No respect, either, you should hear the things they come out with. I'd sooner talk to the blacks, that's the truth, though I know it sounds a strange thing to say. At least they call you missus. Even old Madala knows he can't come into my office without taking his cap off, though heaven help you if you ask that boy to run up to the Greek for a packet of smokes, or round to the Swiss Confectionery. I had a dust-up with him once over it, the old monkey-face, but the manager didn't seem to want to get rid of him, he's been here so long. So he just keeps out of my way and he has his half-crown from me at Christmas, same as the other boys. But you get more sense out of the boss-boy, Jack, than you can out of some whites, believe me, and he can make you laugh, too, in his way – of course they're like children, you see them yelling with laughter over something in their own language, noisy lot of devils; I don't suppose we'd think it funny at all if we knew what it was all about. This Jack used to get a lot of phone calls (I complained to the manager on the quiet and he's put a stop to it, now) and the natives on the other end used to be asking to speak to Mpanza and Makiwane and I don't know what all, and when I'd say there wasn't anyone of that name working here they'd come out with it and ask for Jack. So I said to him one day, why do you people have a hundred and one names, why don't these uncles and aunts and brothers-in-law come out with your name straight away and stop wasting my time? He said, 'Here I'm Jack because Mpanza Makiwane is not a name, and there I'm Mpanza Makiwane because Jack is not a name, but I'm the only one who knows who I am wherever I am.' I couldn't help laughing. He hardly ever calls you missus, I notice, but it doesn't sound cheeky, the way he speaks. Before they were allowed to buy drink for themselves, he used to ask me to buy a bottle of brandy for him once a week and I didn't see any harm.

Even if things are not too bright, no use grumbling. I don't believe in getting old before my time. Now and then it's happened that some man's taken a fancy to me at the garage. Every time he comes to fill up he finds some excuse to talk to me; if a chap likes me, I begin to feel it just like I did when I was seventeen, so that even if he was just sitting in his car looking at me through the glass of the office, I would know that he was waiting for me to come out. Eventually he'd ask me to the hotel for a drink after work. Usually that was as far as it went. I don't know what happens to these blokes, they are married, I suppose, though their wives don't still wear a perfect size fourteen, like I do. They enjoy talking to another woman once in a while, but they quickly get nervous. They are businessmen and well off; one sent me a present, but it was one of those old-fashioned compacts, we used to call them flapjacks, meant for loose powder, and I use the solid kind everyone uses now.

Of course you get some funny types, and, as I say, I'm alone there in the front most of the time, with only the boys, the manager is at head office in town, and the other white men are all at the back. Little while ago a fellow came into my office wanting to pay for his petrol with Rhodesian money. Well, Jack, the boss-boy, came first to tell me that this fellow had given him Rhodesian money. I sent back to say we didn't take it. I looked through the glass and saw a big, expensive American car, not very new, and one of those men you recognize at once as the kind who move about a lot – he was poking out his cheek with his tongue, looking round the station and out into the busy street like, in his head, he was trying to work out his way around in a new town. Some people kick up hell with a native if he refuses them something, but this one didn't seem to; the next thing was he got the boy to bring him to me. 'Boss says he must talk to you,' Jack said, and turned on his heel. But I said, you wait here. I know Johannesburg; my cash-box was there in the open safe. The fellow was young. He had that very tanned skin that has been sunburnt day after day, the tan you see on lifesavers at the beach. His hair was the thick streaky blond kind, waste on men. He says, 'Miss, can't you help me out for half an hour?' Well, I'd had my hair done, it's true, but I don't kid myself you could think of me as a miss unless you saw my figure, from behind. He went on, 'I've just driven down and I haven't had a chance to change my money. Just take this while I get hold of this chap I know and get him to cash a cheque for me.'

I told him there was a bank up the road but he made some excuse. 'I've got to tell my friend I'm in town anyway. Here, I'll leave this – it's a gold one.' And he took the big fancy watch off his arm. 'Go on, please, do me a favour.' Somehow when he smiled he looked not so young, harder. The smile was on the side of his mouth. Anyway, I suddenly said okay, then, and the native boy turned and went out of the office, but I knew it was all right about my cash, and this fellow asked me which was the quickest way to get to Kensington and I came out from behind my desk and looked it up with him on the wall map. I thought he was a fellow of about twenty-nine or thirty; he was so lean, with a snakeskin belt around his hips and a clean white open-neck shirt.

He was back on the dot. I took the money for the petrol and said, here's your watch, pushing it across the counter. I'd seen, the moment he'd gone and I'd picked up the watch to put it in the safe, that it wasn't gold: one of those Jap fakes that men take out of their pockets and try to sell you on streetcorners. But I didn't say anything, because maybe he'd been had? I gave him the benefit of the doubt. What'd it matter? He'd paid for his petrol, anyway. He thanked me and said he supposed he'd better push off and find some hotel. I said the usual sort of thing, was he here on a visit and so on, and he said, yes, he didn't know how long, perhaps a couple of weeks, it all depended, and he'd like somewhere central. We had quite a little chat – you know how it is, you always feel friendly if you've done someone a favour and it's all worked out okay – and I mentioned a couple of hotels. But it's difficult if you don't know what sort of place a person wants, you may send him somewhere too expensive, or on the other hand you might recommend one of the small places that he'd consider just a joint, such as the New Park, near where I live.

A few days later I'd been down to the shops at lunch hour and when I came by where some of the boys were squatting over their lunch in the sun, Jack said, 'That man came again.' Thinks I can read his mind; what man, I said, but they never learn. 'The other day, with the money that was no good.' Oh, you mean the Rhodesian, I said. Jack didn't answer but went on tearing chunks of bread out of half a loaf and stuffing them into his mouth. One of the other boys began telling, in their own language with bits of English thrown in, what I could guess was the story of how the man had tried to pay with money that was no good; big joke, you know; but Jack didn't take any notice, I suppose he'd heard it once too often.

I went into my office to fetch a smoke, and when I was enjoying it outside in the sun Jack came over to the tap near me. I heard him drinking from his hand, and then he said, 'He went and looked in the office window.' Didn't he buy petrol? I said. 'He pulled up at the pump but then he didn't buy, he said he will come back later.' Well, that's all right, what're you getting excited about, we sell people as much petrol as they like, I said. I felt uncomfortable. I don't know why; you'd think I'd been giving away petrol at the garage's expense or something.

'You can't come from Rhodesia on those tyres,' Jack said. No? I said. 'Did you look at those tyres?' Why should *I* look at tyres? 'No-no, you look at those tyres on that old car. You can't drive six hundred miles or so on those tyres. Worn out! Down to the tread!' But who cares where he came from, I said, it's his business. 'But he had that money,' Jack said to me. He shrugged and I shrugged; I went back into my office. As I say, sometimes you find yourself talking to that boy as if he was a white person.

Just before five that same afternoon the fellow came back. I don't know how it was, I happened to look up like I knew the car was going to be there. He was taking petrol and paying for it, this time; old Madala was serving him. I don't know what got into me, curiosity maybe, but I got up and came to my door and said, how's Jo'burg treating you? 'Ah, hell, I've had bad luck,' he says. 'The place I was staying had another booking for my room from today. I was supposed to go to my friend in Berea, but now his wife's brother has come. I don't mind paying for a decent place, but you take one look at some of them . . . Don't you know somewhere?' Well yes, I said, I was telling you that day. And I mentioned the Victoria, but he said he'd tried there, so then I told him about the New Park, near me. He listened, but looking round all the time, his mind was somewhere else. He said, 'They'll tell me they're full, it'll be the same story.' I told him that Mrs Douglas who runs the place is a nice woman – she would be sure to fix him up. 'You couldn't ask her?' he said. I said well, all right, from my place she was only round the corner, I'd pop in on my way home from work and tell her he'd be getting in touch with her.

When he heard that he said he'd give me a lift in his car, and so I took him to Mrs Douglas myself, and she gave him a room. As we walked out of the hotel together he seemed wrapped up in his own affairs again, but on the pavement he suddenly suggested a drink. I thought he meant we'd go into the hotel lounge, but he said, 'I've got a bottle of gin in the car,' and he brought it up to my place. He was telling me about the time he was in the Congo a few years ago, fighting for that native chief, whats's-name – Tshombe – against the Irishmen who were sent out there to put old whats's-name down. The stories he told about Elisabethville! He was paid so much he could live like a king. We only had two gins each out the bottle, but when I wanted him to take it along with him, he said, 'I'll come in for it sometime when I get a chance.' He didn't say anything, but I got the idea he had come up to Jo'burg about a job.

I was frying a slice of liver next evening when he turned up at the door. The bottle was still standing where it'd been left. You feel uncomfortable when the place's full of the smell of frying and anyone can tell you're about to eat. I gave him the bottle but he didn't take it; he said he was on his way to Vereeniging to see someone, he would just have a quick drink. I had to offer him something to eat, with me. He was one of those people who eat without noticing what it is. He never took in the flat, either; I mean he didn't look round at my things the way it's natural you do in someone else's home. And there was a lovely photo of my kid on the built-in fixture round the electric fire. I said to him while we were eating, is it a job you've come down for? He smiled the way youngsters smile at an older person who won't understand, anyway. 'On business.' But you could see that he was not a man who had an office, who wore a suit and sat in a chair. He was like one of those men you see in films, you know, the stranger in town who doesn't look as if he lives anywhere. Somebody in a film, thin and burned red as a brick and not saying much. I mean he did talk but it was never really anything about himself, only about things he'd seen happen. He never asked me anything about myself, either. It was queer; because of this, after I'd seen him a few times, it was just the same as if we were people who know each other so well they don't talk about themselves any more.

Another funny thing was, all the time he was coming in and out the flat, I was talking about him with the boy – with Jack. I don't believe in discussing white people with natives, as a rule, I mean, whatever I think of a white, it encourages disrespect if you talk about it to a black. I've never said anything in front of the boys about the behaviour of that crowd of ducktails in the workshop, for instance. And of course I wouldn't be likely to discuss my private life with a native boy. Jack didn't know that this fellow was coming to the flat, but he'd heard me say I'd fix up about the New Park Hotel, and he'd seen me take a lift home that afternoon. The boy's remark about the tyres seemed to stick in my mind; I said to him: That man came all the way from the Congo.

'In the car?' Jack said; he's got such a serious face, for a native. The car goes all right, I said, he's driving all over with it now.

'Why doesn't he bring it in for retreads?'

I said he was just on holiday, he wouldn't have it done here.

The fellow didn't appear for five or six days and I thought he'd moved on, or made friends, as people do in this town. There was still about two fingers left in his bottle. I don't drink when I'm on my own. Again I meant to look at the tyres for myself, but I forgot. He took me home just like it had been an arranged thing; you know, a grown-up son calling for his mother not because he wants to, but because he has to. We hardly spoke in the car. I went out for pies, which wasn't much of a dinner to offer anyone, but, as I say, he didn't know what he was eating, and he didn't want the gin, he had some cans of beer in the car. He leaned his chair back with all the weight on two legs and said, 'I think I must clear out of this lousy dump, I don't know what you've got to be to get along here with these sharks.' I said, you kids give up too easy, have you still not landed a job? 'A job!' he said. 'They owe me *money*, I'm trying to get *money* out of them.' What's it all about, I said, what money? He didn't take any notice, as if I wouldn't understand. 'Smart alecks and swindlers. I been here nearly three lousy weeks, now.' I said, everybody who comes here finds Jo'burg tough compared with their home.

He'd had his head tipped back and he lifted it straight and looked at me. 'I'm not such a kid.' No? I said, feeling a bit awkward because he never talked about himself before. He was looking at me all the time, you'd have thought he was going to find his age written on my face. 'I'm thirty-seven,' he said. 'Did you know that? Thirty-seven. Not so much younger.'

Forty-nine. It was true, not so much. But he looked so young, with that hair always slicked back longish behind the ears as if he'd just come out of the shower, and that brown neck in the open-neck shirt. Lean men wear well, you can't tell. He did have false teeth, though, that was why his mouth made him look hard. I supposed he could have been thirty-seven; I didn't know, I didn't know.

It was like the scars on his body. There were scars on his back and other scars on his stomach, and my heart was in my mouth for him when I saw them, still pink and raw-looking, but he said that the ones on his back were from strokes he'd had in a boys' home as a kid and the others were from the fighting in Katanga.

I know nobody would believe me, they would think I was just trying to make excuses for myself, but in the morning everything seemed just the same, I didn't feel I knew him any better. It was just like it was that first day when he came in with his Rhodesian money. He said, 'Leave me the key. I might as well use the place while you're out all day.' But what about the hotel, I said. 'I've taken my things,' he says. I said, you mean you've moved out? And something in his face, the bored sort of look, made me ask, you've told Mrs Douglas? 'She's found out by now,' he said, it was unusual for him to smile. You mean you went without paying? I said. 'Look, I told you I can't get my money out of those bastards.'

Well, what could I do? I'd taken him to Mrs Douglas myself. The woman'd given him a room on my recommendation. I had to go over to the New Park and spin her some yarn about him having to leave suddenly and that he'd left the money for me to pay. What else could I do? Of course I didn't tell *him*.

But I told Jack. That's the funny thing about it. I told Jack that the man had disappeared, run off without paying my friend who ran the hotel where he was staying. The boy clicked his tongue the way they do, and laughed. And I said that was what you got for trying to help people. Yes, he said, Johannesburg was full of people like that, but you learn to know their faces, even if they were nice faces.

I said, you think that man had a nice face?

'You see he has a nice face,' the boy said.

I was afraid I'd find the fellow there when I got home, and he was there. I said to him, that's my daughter, and showed him the photo, but he took no interest, not even when I said she lived in Gwelo and perhaps he knew the town himself. I said why didn't he go back to Rhodesia to his job but he said Central Africa was finished, he wasn't going to be pushed around by a lot of blacks running the show – from what he told me, it's awful, you can't keep them out of hotels or anything.

Later on he went out to get some smokes and I suddenly thought, I'll lock the door and I won't let him into the flat again. I had made up my mind to do it. But when I saw his shadow on the other side of the frosty glass I just got up and opened it, and I felt like a fool, what was there to be afraid of? He was such a clean, good-looking fellow standing there; and anybody can be down on his luck. I sometimes wonder what'll happen to me – in some years, of course – if I can't work any more and I'm alone here, and nobody comes. Every Sunday you read in the paper about women dead alone in flats, no one discovers it for days.

He smoked night and day, like the world had some bad smell that he had to keep out of his nose. He was smoking in the bed at the weekend and I made a remark about Princess Margaret when she was here as a kid in 1947 – I was looking at a story about the Royal Family, in the Sunday paper. He said he supposed he'd seen her, it was the year he went to the boys' home and they were taken to watch the procession.

One of the few things he'd told me about himself was that he was eight when he was sent to the home; I lay there and worked out that if he was thirty-seven, he should have been twenty in 1947, not eight years old.

But by then I found it hard to believe that he was only twenty-five. You could always get rid of a boy of twenty-five. He wouldn't have the strength inside to make you afraid to try it.

I'd've felt safer if someone had known about him and me but of course I couldn't talk to anyone. Imagine the Versfelds. Or the woman I go out with on Fridays, I don't think she's had a cup of tea with a man since her husband died! I remarked to Jack, the boss-boy, how old did he think the man had been, the one with the Rhodesian money who cheated the hotel? He said, 'He's still here?' I said no, no, I just wondered. 'He's young, that one,' he said, but I should have remembered that half the time natives don't know their own age, it doesn't matter to them the way it does to us. I said to him, wha'd'you call young? He jerked his head back at the workshop. 'Same like the mechanics.' That bunch of kids! But this fellow wasn't cocky like them, wrestling with each other all over the place, calling after girls, fancying themselves the Beatles when they sing in the washroom. The people he used to go off to see about things – I never saw any of them. If he had friends, they never came round. If only *somebody* else had known he was in the flat!

Then he said he was having the car overhauled because he was going off to Durban. He said he had to leave the next Saturday. So I felt much better; I also felt bad, in a way, because there I'd been, thinking I'd have to find some way to make him go. He put his hand on my waist, in the daylight, and smiled right out at me and said, 'Sorry; got to push on and get moving sometime, you know,' and it was true that in a way he was right, I couldn't think what it'd be like without him, though I was always afraid he would stay. Oh he was nice to me then, I can tell you; he could be nice if he wanted to, it was like a trick that he could do, so real you couldn't believe it when it stopped just like that. I told him he should've brought the car into our place, I'd've seen to it that they did a proper job on it, but no, a friend of his was doing it free, in his own workshop.

Saturday came, he didn't go. The car wasn't ready. He sat about most of the week, disappeared for a night, but was there again in the morning. I'd given him a couple of quid to keep him going. I said to him, what are you mucking about with that car in somebody's back yard for? Take it to a decent garage. Then – I'll never forget it – cool as anything, a bit irritated, he said, 'Forget it. I haven't got the car any more.' I said, wha'd'you mean, you mean you've sold it? – I suppose because in the back of my mind I'd been thinking, why doesn't he sell it, he needs money. And he said, 'That's right. It's sold,' but I knew he was lying, he couldn't be bothered to think of anything else to say. Once he'd said the car was sold, he said he was waiting for the money; he did pay me back three quid, but he borrowed again a day or so later. He'd keep his back to me when I came into the flat and he wouldn't answer when I spoke to him; and then just when he turned on me with that closed, half-asleep face and I'd think, this is it, now this is it – I can't explain how finished, done-for I felt, I only know that he had on his face exactly the same look I remember on the face of a man, once, who was drowning some kittens one after the other in a bucket of water – just as I knew it was coming, he would burst out laughing at me. It was the only time he laughed. He would laugh until, nearly crying, I would begin to laugh too. And we would pretend it was kidding, and he would be nice to me, oh, he would be nice to me.

I used to sit in my office at the garage and look round at the car adverts and the maps on the wall and my elephant ear growing in the oil drum and that was the only place I felt: but this is nonsense, what's got into me? The flat, and him in it – they didn't seem real. Then I'd go home at five and there it would all be.

I said to Jack, what's a '59 Chrysler worth? He took his time, he was cleaning his hands on some cotton waste. He said, 'With those tyres, nobody will pay much.'

Just to show him that he mustn't get too free with a white person, I asked him to send up to Mr Levine for a headache powder for me. I joked, I'm getting a bit like old Madala there, I feel so tired today.

D'you know what that boy said to me then? They've got more feeling than whites sometimes, that's the truth. He said, 'When my children grow up they must work for me. Why don't you live there in Rhodesia with your daughter? The child must look after the mother. Why must you stay here alone in this town?'

Of course I wasn't going to explain to him that I like my independence. I always say I hope when I get old I die before I become a burden on anybody. But that afternoon I did something I should've done long ago, I said to the boy, if ever I don't turn up to work, you must tell them in the workshop to send someone to my flat to look for me. And I wrote down the address. Days could go by before anyone'd find what had become of me; it's not right.

When I got home that same evening, the fellow wasn't there. He'd gone. Not a word, not a note; nothing. Every time I heard the lift rattling I thought, here he is. But he didn't come. When I was home on Saturday afternoon I couldn't stand it any longer and I went up to the Versfelds and asked the old lady if I couldn't sleep there a few days, I said my flat was being painted and the smell turned my stomach. I thought, if he comes to the garage, there are people around, at least there are the boys. I was smoking nearly as much as *he* used to and I couldn't sleep. I had to ask Mr Levine to give me something. The slightest sound and I was in a cold sweat. At the end of the week I had to go back to the flat, and I bought a chain for the door and made a heavy curtain so's you couldn't see anyone standing there. I didn't go out, once I'd got in from work – not even to the early flicks – so I wouldn't have to come back into the building at night. You know how it is when you're nervous, the funniest things comfort you: I'd just tell myself, well, if I shouldn't turn up to work in the morning, the boy'd send someone to see.

Then slowly I was beginning to forget about it. I kept the curtain and the chain and I stayed at home, but when you get used to something, no matter what it is, you don't think about it all the time, any more, though you still believe you do. I hadn't been to Maison Claude for about two weeks and my hair was a sight. Claude advised a soft perm and so it happened that I took a couple of hours off in the afternoon to get it done. The boss-boy Jack says to me when I come back, 'He was here.'

I didn't know what to do, I couldn't help staring quickly all round. When, I said. 'Now-now, while you were out.' I had the feeling I couldn't get away. I knew he would come up to me with that closed, half-asleep face – burned as a good-looker lifesaver, burned like one of those tramps who are starving and lousy and pickled with cheap booze but have a horrible healthy look that comes from having nowhere to go out of the sun. I don't know what that boy must have thought of me, my face. He said, 'I told him you're gone. You don't work here any more. You went to Rhodesia to your daughter. I don't know which place.' And he put his nose back in one of the newspapers he's always reading whenever things are slack; I think he fancies himself quite the educated man and he likes to read about all these blacks who are becoming prime ministers and so on in other countries these days. I never remark on it; if you take any notice of things like that with them, you begin to give them big ideas about themselves.

That fellow's never bothered me again. I never breathed a word to anybody about it – as I say, that's the trouble when you work alone in an office like I do, there's no one you can speak to. It just shows you, a woman on her own has always got to look out; it's not only that it's not safe to walk about alone at night because of the natives, this whole town is full of people you can't trust.

A Chip of Glass Ruby

When the duplicating machine was brought into the house, Bamjee said, 'Isn't it enough that you've got the Indians' troubles on your back?' Mrs Bamjee said, with a smile that showed the gap of a missing tooth but was confident all the same, 'What's the difference, Yusuf? We've all got the same troubles.'

'Don't tell me that. We don't have to carry passes; let the natives protest against passes on their own, there are millions of them. Let them go ahead with it.'

The nine Bamjee and Pahad children were present at this exchange as they were always; in the small house that held them all there was no room for privacy for the discussion of matters they were too young to hear, and so they had never been too young to hear anything. Only their sister and half-sister, Girlie, was missing; she was the eldest, and married. The children looked expectantly, unalarmed and interested, at Bamjee, who had neither left the room nor settled down again to the task of rolling his own cigarettes, which had been interrupted by the arrival of the duplicator. He had looked at the thing that had come hidden in a wash-basket and conveyed in a black man's taxi, and the children turned on it too, their black eyes surrounded by thick lashes like those still, open flowers with hairy tentacles that close on whatever touches them.

'A fine thing to have on the table where we eat,' was all he said at last. They smelled the machine among them; a smell of cold black grease. He went out, heavily on tiptoe, in his troubled way.

'It's going to go nicely on the sideboard!' Mrs Bamjee was busy making a place by removing the two pink glass vases filled with plastic carnations and the hand-painted velvet runner with the picture of the Taj Mahal.

After supper she began to run off leaflets on the machine. The family lived in that room – the three other rooms in the house were full of beds – and they were all there. The older children shared a bottle of ink while they did their homework, and the two little ones pushed a couple of empty milk-bottles in and out the chair-legs. The three-year-old fell asleep and was carted away by one of the girls. They all drifted off to bed eventually; Bamjee himself went before the older children – he was a fruit-and-vegetable hawker and was up at half past four every morning to get to the market by five. 'Not long now,' said Mrs Bamjee. The older children looked up and smiled at him. He turned his back on her. She still wore the traditional clothing of a Moslem woman, and her body, which was scraggy and unimportant as a dress on a peg when it was not host to a child, was wrapped in the trailing rags of a cheap sari and her thin black plait was greased. When she was a girl, in the Transvaal town where they lived still, her mother fixed a chip of glass ruby in her nostril; but she had abandoned that adornment as too old-style, even for her, long ago.

She was up until long after midnight, turning out leaflets. She did it as if she might have been pounding chillies.

Bamjee did not have to ask what the leaflets were. He had read the papers. All the past week Africans had been destroying their passes and then presenting themselves for arrest. Their leaders were jailed on charges of incitement, campaign offices were raided – someone must be helping the few minor leaders who were left to keep the campaign going without offices or equipment. What was it the leaflets would say – 'Don't go to work tomorrow', 'Day of Protest', 'Burn Your Pass for Freedom'? He didn't want to see.

He was used to coming home and finding his wife sitting at the table deep in discussion with strangers or people whose names were familiar by repute. Some were prominent Indians, like the lawyer, Dr Abdul Mohammed Khan, or the big businessman, Mr Moonsamy Patel, and he was flattered, in a suspicious way, to meet them in his house. As he came home from work next day he met Dr Khan coming out of the house and Dr Khan – a highly educated man – said to him, 'A wonderful woman.' But Bamjee had never caught his wife out in any presumption; she behaved properly, as any Moslem woman should, and once her business with such gentlemen was over would never, for instance, have sat down to eat with them. He found her now back in the kitchen, setting about the preparation of dinner and carrying on a conversation on several different wave-lengths with the children. 'It's really a shame if you're tired of lentils, Jimmy, because that's what you're getting – Amina, hurry up, get a pot of water going – don't worry, I'll mend that in a minute, just bring the yellow cotton, and there's a needle in the cigarette box on the sideboard.'

'Was that Dr Khan leaving?' said Bamjee.

'Yes, there's going to be a stay-at-home on Monday. Desai's ill, and he's got to get the word around by himself. Bob Jali was up all last night printing leaflets, but he's gone to have a tooth out.' She had always treated Bamjee as if it were only a mannerism that made him appear uninterested in politics, the way some woman will persist in interpreting her husband's bad temper as an endearing gruffness hiding boundless goodwill, and she talked to him of these things just as she passed on to him neighbours' or family gossip.

'What for do you want to get mixed up with these killings

and stonings and I don't know what? Congress should keep out of it. Isn't it enough with the Group Areas?'

She laughed. 'Now, Yusuf, you know you don't believe that. Look how you said the same thing when the Group Areas started in Natal. You said we should begin to worry when we get moved out of our own houses here in the Transvaal. And then your own mother lost her house in Noorddorp, and there you are; you saw that nobody's safe. Oh, Girlie was here this afternoon, she says Ismail's brother's engaged – that's nice, isn't it? His mother will be pleased; she was worried.'

'Why was she worried?' asked Jimmy, who was fifteen, and old enough to patronize his mother.

'Well, she wanted to see him settled. There's a party on Sunday week at Ismail's place – you'd better give me your suit to give to the cleaners tomorrow, Yusuf.'

One of the girls presented herself at once. 'I'll have nothing to wear, Ma.'

Mrs Bamjee scratched her sallow face. 'Perhaps Girlie will lend you her pink, eh? Run over to Girlie's place now and say I say will she lend it to you.'

The sound of commonplaces often does service as security, and Bamjee, going to sit in the armchair with the shiny arm-rests that was wedged between the table and the side-board, lapsed into an unthinking doze that, like all times of dreamlike ordinariness during those weeks, was filled with uneasy jerks and starts back into reality. The next morning, as soon as he got to market, he heard that Dr Khan had been arrested. But that night Mrs Bamjee sat up making a new dress for her daughter; the sight disarmed Bamjee, reassured him again, against his will, so that the resentment he had been making ready all day faded into a morose and accusing silence. Heaven knew, of course, who came and went in the house during the day. Twice in that week of riots, raids and arrests, he found black women in the house when he came home; plain ordinary native women in doeks, drinking tea. This was not a thing other Indian women would have in their homes, he thought bitterly; but then his wife was not like other people, in a way he could not put his finger on, except to say what it was not: not scandalous, not punishable, not rebellious. It was, like the attraction that had led him to marry her, Pahad's widow with five children, something he could not see clearly.

When the Special Branch knocked steadily on the door in the small hours of Thursday morning he did not wake up, for his return to consciousness was always set in his mind to half past four, and that was more than an hour away. Mrs Bamjee got up herself, struggled into Jimmy's raincoat which was hanging over a chair and went to the front door. The clock on the wall – a wedding present when she married Pahad – showed three o'clock when she snapped on the light, and she knew at once who it was on the other side of the door. Although she was not surprised, her hands shook like a very old person's as she undid the locks and the complicated catch on the wire burglar-proofing. And then she opened the door and they were there – two coloured policemen in plain clothes. 'Zanip Bamjee?'

'Yes.'

As they talked, Bamjee woke up in the sudden terror of having overslept. Then he became conscious of men's voices. He heaved himself out of bed in the dark and went to the window, which, like the front door, was covered with a heavy mesh of thick wire against intruders from the dingy lane it looked upon. Bewildered, he appeared in the room, where the policemen were searching through a soapbox of papers beside the duplicating machine. 'Yusuf, it's for me,' Mrs Bamjee said.

At once, the snap of a trap, realization came. He stood there in an old shirt before the two policemen, and the woman was going off to prison because of the natives. 'There you are!' he shouted, standing away from her. 'That's what you've got for it. Didn't I tell you? Didn't I? That's the end of it now. That's the finish. That's what it's come to.' She listened with her head at the slightest tilt to one side, as if to ward off a blow, or in compassion.

Jimmy, Pahad's son, appeared at the door with a suitcase; two or three of the girls were behind him. 'Here, Ma, you take my green jersey.' 'I've found your clean blouse.' Bamjee had to keep moving out of their way as they helped their mother to make ready. It was like the preparation for one of the family festivals his wife made such a fuss over; wherever he put himself, they bumped into him. Even the two policemen mumbled, 'Excuse me,' and pushed past into the rest of the house to continue their search. They took with them a tome that Nehru had written in prison; it had been bought from a persevering travelling salesman and kept, for years, on the mantelpiece. 'Oh, don't take that, please,' Mrs Bamjee said suddenly, clinging to the arm of the man who had picked it up.

The man held it away from her.

'What does it matter, Ma?'

It was true that no one in the house had ever read it; but she said, 'It's for my children.'

'Ma, leave it.' Jimmy, who was squat and plump, looked like a merchant advising a client against a roll of silk she had set her heart on. She went into the bedroom and got dressed. When she came out in her old yellow sari with a brown coat over it, the faces of the children were behind her like faces on the platform of a railway station. They kissed her good-bye. The policemen did not hurry her, but she seemed to be in a hurry just the same.

'What am I going to do?' Bamjee accused them all.

The policemen looked away patiently.

'It'll be all right. Girlie will help. The big children can

manage. And Yusuf –' The children crowded in around her; two of the younger ones had awakened and appeared, asking shrill questions.

'Come on,' said the policemen.

'I want to speak to my husband.' She broke away and came back to him, and the movement of her sari hid them from the rest of the room for a moment. His face hardened in suspicious anticipation against the request to give some message to the next fool who would take up her pamphleteering until he, too, was arrested. 'On Sunday,' she said. 'Take them on Sunday.' He did not know what she was talking about. 'The engagement party,' she whispered, low and urgent. 'They shouldn't miss it. Ismail will be offended.'

They listened to the car drive away. Jimmy bolted and barred the front door, and then at once opened it again; he put on the raincoat that his mother had taken off. 'Going to tell Girlie,' he said. The children went back to bed. Their father did not say a word to any of them; their talk, the crying of the younger ones and the argumentative voices of the older, went on in the bedrooms. He found himself alone; he felt the night all around him. And then he happened to meet the clock face and saw with a terrible sense of unfamiliarity that this was not the secret night but an hour he should have recognized: the time he always got up. He pulled on his trousers and his dirty white hawker's coat and wound his grey muffler up to the stubble on his chin and went to work.

The duplicating machine was gone from the sideboard. The policemen had taken it with them, along with the pamphlets and the conference reports and the stack of old newspapers that had collected on top of the wardrobe in the bedroom – not the thick dailies of the white men but the thin, impermanent-looking papers that spoke up, sometimes interrupted by suppression or lack of money, for the rest. It was all gone. When he had married her and moved in with her and her five children, into what had been the Pahad and became the Bamjee house, he had not recognized the humble, harmless and apparently useless routine tasks – the minutes of meetings being written up on the dining-room table at night, the government blue books that were read while the latest baby was suckled, the employment of the fingers of the older children in the fashioning of crinkle-paper Congress rosettes – as activity intended to move mountains. For years and years he had not noticed it, and now it was gone.

The house was quiet. The children kept to their lairs, crowded on the beds with the doors shut. He sat and looked at the sideboard, where the plastic carnations and the mat with the picture of the Taj Mahal were in place. For the first few weeks he never spoke of her. There was the feeling, in the house, that he had wept and raged at her, that boulders of reproach had thundered down upon her absence, and yet he had said not one word. He had not been to inquire where she was; Jimmy and Girlie had gone to Mohammed Ebrahim, the lawyer, and when he found out that their mother had been taken – when she was arrested, at least – to a prison in the next town, they had stood about outside the big prison door for hours while they waited to be told where she had been moved from there. At last they had discovered that she was fifty miles away, in Pretoria. Jimmy asked Bamjee for five shillings to help Girlie pay the train fare to Pretoria, once she had been interviewed by the police and had been given a permit to visit her mother; he put three two-shilling pieces on the table for Jimmy to pick up, and the boy, looking at him keenly, did not know whether the extra shilling meant anything, or whether it was merely that Bamjee had no change.

It was only when relations and neighbours came to the house that Bamjee would suddenly begin to talk. He had never been so expansive in his life as he was in the company of these visitors, many of them come on a polite call rather in the nature of a visit of condolence. 'Ah, yes, yes, you can see how I am – you see what has been done to me. Nine children, and I am on the cart all day. I get home at seven or eight. What are you to do? What can people like us do?'

'Poor Mrs Bamjee. Such a kind lady.'

'Well, you see for yourself. They walk in here in the middle of the night and leave a houseful of children. I'm out on the cart all day, I've got a living to earn.' Standing about in his shirt sleeves, he became quite animated; he would call for the girls to bring fruit drinks for the visitors. When they were gone, it was as if he, who was orthodox if not devout and never drank liquor, had been drunk and abruptly sobered up; he looked dazed and could not have gone over in his mind what he had been saying. And as he cooled, the lump of resentment and wrongedness stopped his throat again.

Bamjee found one of the little boys the centre of a self-important group of championing brothers and sisters in the room one evening, 'They've been cruel to Ahmed.'

'What has he done?' said the father.

'Nothing! Nothing!' The little girl stood twisting her handkerchief excitedly.

An older one, thin as her mother, took over, silencing the others with a gesture of her skinny hand. 'They did it at school today. They made an example of him.'

'What is an example?' said Bamjee impatiently.

'The teacher made him come up and stand in front of the whole class, and he told them, "You see this boy? His mother's in jail because she likes the natives so much. She wants the Indians to be the same as natives." '

'It's terrible,' he said. His hands fell to his sides. 'Did she ever think of this?'

'That's why Ma's *there*,' said Jimmy, putting aside his comic and emptying out his schoolbooks upon the table. 'That's all the kids need to know. Ma's there because things like this happen. Petersen's a coloured teacher, and it's his black blood that's brought him trouble all his life, I suppose. He hates anyone who says everybody's the same because that takes away from him his bit of whiteness that's all he's got. What d'you expect? It's nothing to make too much fuss about.'

'Of course, you are fifteen and you know everything,' Bamjee mumbled at him.

'I don't say that. But I know Ma, anyway.' The boy laughed.

There was a hunger strike among the political prisoners, and Bamjee could not bring himself to ask Girlie if her mother was starving herself too. He would not ask; and yet he saw in the young woman's face the gradual weakening of her mother. When the strike had gone on for nearly a week one of the elder children burst into tears at the table and could not eat. Bamjee pushed his own plate away in rage.

Sometimes he spoke out loud to himself while he was driving the vegetable lorry. 'What for?' Again and again: 'What for?' She was not a modern woman who cut her hair and wore short skirts. He had married a good plain Moslem woman who bore children and stamped her own chillies. He had a sudden vision of her at the duplicating machine, that night just before she was taken away, and he felt himself maddened, baffled and hopeless. He had become the ghost of a victim, hanging about the scene of a crime whose motive he could not understand and had not had time to learn.

The hunger strike at the prison went into the second week. Alone in the rattling cab of his lorry, he said things that he heard as if spoken by someone else, and his heart burned in fierce agreement with them. 'For a crowd of natives who'll smash our shops and kill us in our houses when their time comes.' 'She will starve herself to death there.' 'She will die there.' 'Devils who will burn and kill us.' He fell into bed each night like a stone, and dragged himself up in the mornings as a beast of burden is beaten to its feet.

One of these mornings, Girlie appeared very early, while he was wolfing bread and strong tea – alternate sensations of dry solidity and stinging heat – at the kitchen table. Her real name was Fatima, of course, but she had adopted the silly modern name along with the clothes of the young factory girls among whom she worked. She was expecting her first baby in a week or two, and her small face, her cut and curled hair and the sooty arches drawn over her eyebrows did not seem to belong to her thrust-out body under a clean smock. She wore mauve lipstick and was smiling her cocky little white girl's smile, foolish and bold, not like an Indian girl's at all.

'What's the matter?' he said.

She smiled again. 'Don't you know? I told Bobby he must get me up in time this morning. I wanted to be sure I wouldn't miss you today.'

'I don't know what you're talking about.'

She came over and put her arm up around his unwilling neck and kissed the grey bristles at the side of his mouth. 'Many happy returns! Don't you know it's your birthday?'

'No,' he said. 'I didn't know, didn't think –' He broke the pause by swiftly picking up the bread and giving his attention desperately to eating and drinking. His mouth was busy, but his eyes looked at her, intensely black. She said nothing, but stood there with him. She would not speak, and at last he said, swallowing a piece of bread that tore at his throat as it went down, 'I don't remember these things.'

The girl nodded, the Woolworth baubles in her ears swinging. 'That's the first thing she told me when I saw her yesterday – don't forget it's Bajie's birthday tomorrow.'

He shrugged over it. 'It means a lot to children. But that's how she is. Whether it's one of the old cousins or the neighbour's grandmother, she always knows when the birthday is. What importance is my birthday, while she's sitting there in a prison? I don't understand how she can do the things she does when her mind is always full of woman's nonsense at the same time – that's what I don't understand with her.'

'Oh, but don't you see?' the girl said. 'It's because she doesn't want anybody to be left out. It's because she always remembers; remembers everything – people without somewhere to live, hungry kids, boys who can't get educated – remembers all the time. That's how Ma is.'

'Nobody else is like that.' It was half a complaint.

'No, nobody else,' said his stepdaughter.

She sat herself down at the table, resting her belly. He put his head in his hands. 'I'm getting old' – but he was overcome by something much more curious, by an answer. He knew why he had desired her, the ugly widow with five children; he knew what way it was in which she was not like the others; it was there, like the fact of the belly that lay between him and her daughter.

City Lovers

Dr Franz-Josef von Leinsdorf is a geologist absorbed in his work; wrapped up in it, as the saying goes – year after year the experience of this work enfolds him, swaddling him away from the landscapes, the cities and the people, wherever he lives: Peru, New Zealand, the United States. He's always been like that, his mother could confirm from their native Austria. There, even as a handsome small boy he presented only his profile to her: turned away to his bits of rock and stone. His few relaxations have not changed much since then. An occasional skiing trip, listening to music, reading poetry – Rainer Maria Rilke once stayed in his grandmother's hunting lodge in the forests of Styria and the boy was introduced to Rilke's poems while very young.

Layer upon layer, country after country, wherever his work takes him – and now he has been almost seven years in Africa. First the Côte d'Ivoire, and for the past five years, South Africa. The shortage of skilled manpower brought about his recruitment here. He has no interest in the politics of the countries he works in. His private preoccupation-within-the-preoccupation of his work has been research into underground water-courses, but the mining company that employs him in a senior though not executive capacity is interested only in mineral discovery. So he is much out in the field – which is the veld, here – seeking new gold, copper, platinum and uranium deposits. When he is at home – on this particular job, in this particular country, this city – he lives in a two-roomed flat in a suburban block with a landscaped garden, and does his shopping at a supermarket conveniently across the street. He is not married – yet. That is how his colleagues, and the typists and secretaries at the mining company's head office, would define his situation. Both men and women would describe him as a good-looking man, in a foreign way, with the lower half of the face dark and middle-aged (his mouth is thin and curving, and no matter how close-shaven his beard shows like fine shot embedded in the skin round mouth and chin) and the upper half contradictorily young, with deep-set eyes (some would say grey, some black), thick eyelashes and brows. A tangled gaze: through which concentration and gleaming thoughtfulness perhaps appear as fire and languor. It is this that the women in the office mean when they remark he's not unattractive. Although the gaze seems to promise, he has never invited any one of them to go out with him. There is the general assumption he probably has a girl who's been picked for him, he's bespoken by one of his own kind, back home in Europe where he comes from. Many of these well-educated Europeans have no intention of becoming permanent immigrants; neither the remnant of white colonial life nor idealistic involvement with Black Africa appeals to them.

One advantage, at least, of living in underdeveloped or half-developed countries is that flats are serviced. All Dr von Leinsdorf has to do for himself is buy his own supplies and cook an evening meal if he doesn't want to go to a restaurant. It is simply a matter of dropping in to the supermarket on his way from his car to his flat after work in the afternoon. He wheels a trolley up and down the shelves, and his simple needs are presented to him in the form of tins, packages, plastic-wrapped meat, cheeses, fruit and vegetables, tubes, bottles . . . At the cashier's counters where customers must converge and queue there are racks of small items uncategorized, for last-minute purchase. Here, as the coloured girl cashier punches the adding machine, he picks up cigarettes and perhaps a packet of salted nuts or a bar of nougat. Or razor-blades, when he remembers he's running short. One evening in winter he saw that the cardboard display was empty of the brand of blades he preferred, and he drew the cashier's attention to this. These young coloured girls are usually pretty helpful, taking money and punching their machines in a manner that asserts with the time-serving obstinacy of the half-literate the limit of any responsibility towards customers, but this one ran an alert glance over the selection of razor-blades, apologized that she was not allowed to leave her post, and said she would see that the stock was replenished 'next time'. A day or two later she recognized him, gravely, as he took his turn before her counter – 'I ahssed them, but it's out of stock. You can't get it. I did ahss about it.' He said this didn't matter. 'When it comes in, I can keep a few packets for you.' He thanked her.

He was away with the prospectors the whole of the next week. He arrived back in town just before nightfall on Friday, and was on his way from car to flat with his arms full of briefcase, suitcase and canvas bags when someone stopped him by standing timidly in his path. He was about to dodge round unseeingly on the crowded pavement but she spoke. 'We got the blades in now. I didn't see you in the shop this week, but I kept some for when you come. So . . .'

He recognized her. He had never seen her standing before, and she was wearing a coat. She was rather small and finely made, for one of them. The coat was skimpy but no big backside jutted. The cold brought an apricot-graining of warm colour to her cheekbones, beneath which a very small face was quite delicately hollowed, and the skin was smooth, the subdued satiny colour of certain yellow wood. That crêpey hair, but worn drawn back flat and in a little knot pushed into one of the cheap wool chignons that (he recognized also) hung in the miscellany of small goods along with the razor-blades, at the supermarket. He said thanks, he was in a hurry, he'd only just got back from a trip – shifting the burdens he carried, to demonstrate. 'Oh shame.' She acknowledged his load. 'But if you want I can run in and get it for you quickly. If you want.'

He saw at once it was perfectly clear that all the girl meant was that she would go back to the supermarket, buy the blades and bring the packet to him there where he stood, on the pavement. And it seemed that it was this certainty that made him say, in the kindly tone of assumption used for an obliging underling, 'I live just across there – *Atlantis* – that flat building. Could you drop them by, for me – number seven-hundred-and-eighteen, seventh floor –'

She had not before been inside one of these big flat buildings near where she worked. She lived a bus- and train-ride away to the West of the city, but this side of the black townships, in a township for people her tint. There was a pool with ferns, not plastic, and even a little waterfall pumped electrically over rocks, in the entrance of the building *Atlantis*; she didn't wait for the lift marked GOODS but took the one meant for whites and a white woman with one of those sausage-dogs on a lead got in with her but did not pay her any attention. The corridors leading to the flats were nicely glassed-in, not draughty.

He wondered if he should give her a twenty-cent piece for her trouble – ten cents would be right for a black; but she said, 'Oh no – please, here –' standing outside his open door and awkwardly pushing back at his hand the change from the money he'd given her for the razor-blades. She was smiling, for the first time, in the dignity of refusing a tip. It was difficult to know how to treat these people, in this country; to know what they expected. In spite of her embarrassing refusal of the coin, she stood there, completely unassuming, fists thrust down the pockets of her cheap coat against the cold she'd come in from, rather pretty thin legs neatly aligned, knee to knee, ankle to ankle.

'Would you like a cup of coffee or something?'

He couldn't very well take her into his study-cum-living-room and offer her a drink. She followed him to his kitchen, but at the sight of her pulling out the single chair to drink her cup of coffee at the kitchen table, he said, 'No – bring it in here –' and led the way into the big room where, among his books and his papers, his files of scientific correspondence (and the cigar boxes of stamps from the envelopes), his racks of records, his specimens of minerals and rocks, he lived alone.

It was no trouble to her; she saved him the trips to the supermarket and brought him his groceries two or three times a week. All he had to do was to leave a list and the key under the doormat, and she would come up in her lunch-hour to collect them, returning to put his supplies in the flat after work. Sometimes he was home and sometimes not. He bought a box of chocolates and left it, with a note, for her to find; and that was acceptable, apparently, as a gratuity.

Her eyes went over everything in the flat although her body tried to conceal its sense of being out of place by remaining as still as possible, holding its contours in the chair offered her as a stranger's coat is set aside and remains exactly as left until the owner takes it up to go. 'You collect?'

'Well, these are specimens – connected with my work.'

'My brother used to collect. Miniatures. With brandy and whisky and that, in them. From all over. Different countries.'

The second time she watched him grinding coffee for the cup he had offered her she said, 'You always do that? Always when you make coffee?'

'But of course. Is it no good, for you? Do I make it too strong?'

'Oh it's just I'm not used to it. We buy it ready – you know, it's in a bottle, you just add a bit to the milk or water.'

He laughed, instructive: 'That's not coffee, that's a synthetic flavouring. In my country we drink only real coffee, fresh, from the beans – you smell how good it is as it's being ground?'

She was stopped by the caretaker and asked what she wanted in the building? Heavy with the *bona fides* of groceries clutched to her body, she said she was working at number 718, on the seventh floor. The caretaker did not tell her not to use the whites' lift; after all, she was not black; her family was very light-skinned.

There was the item 'grey button for trousers' on one of his shopping lists. She said as she unpacked the supermarket carrier 'Give me the pants, so long, then,' and sat on his sofa that was always gritty with fragments of pipe tobacco, sewing in and out through the four holes of the button with firm, fluent movements of the right hand, gestures supplying the articulacy missing from her talk. She had a little yokel's, peasant's (he thought of it) gap between her two front teeth when she smiled that he didn't much like, but, face ellipsed to three-quarter angle, eyes cast down in concentration with soft lips almost closed, this didn't matter. He said, watching her sew, 'You're a good girl'; and touched her.

She remade the bed every late afternoon when they left it and she dressed again before she went home. After a week there was a day when late afternoon became evening, and they were still in the bed.

'Can't you stay the night?'

'My mother,' she said.

'Phone her. Make an excuse.' He was a foreigner. He had been in the country five years, but he didn't understand that people don't usually have telephones in their houses, where she lived. She got up to dress. He didn't want that tender body to go out in the night cold and kept hindering her with the interruption of his hands; saying nothing. Before she put on her coat, when the body had already disappeared, he spoke. 'But you must make some arrangement.'

'Oh my mother!' Her face opened to fear and vacancy he could not read.

He was not entirely convinced the woman would think of her daughter as some pure and unsullied virgin . . . 'Why?'

The girl said, 'S'e'll be scared. S'e'll be scared we get caught.'

'Don't tell her anything. Say I'm employing you.' In this country he was working in now there were generally rooms on the roofs of flat buildings for tenants' servants.

She said: 'That's what I told the caretaker.'

She ground fresh coffee beans every time he wanted a cup while he was working at night. She never attempted to cook anything until she had watched in silence while he did it the way he liked, and she learned to reproduce exactly the simple dishes he preferred. She handled his pieces of rock and stone, at first admiring the colours – 'It'd make a beautiful ring or a necklace, ay.' Then he showed her the striations, for formation of each piece, and explained what each was, and how, in the long life of the earth, it had been formed. He named the mineral it yielded, and what that was used for. He worked at his papers, writing, writing, every night, so it did not matter that they could not go out together to public places. On Sundays she got into his car in the basement garage and they drove to the country and picnicked away up in the Magaliesberg, where there was no one. He read or poked about among the rocks; they climbed together, to the mountain pools. He taught her to swim. She had never seen the sea. She squealed and shrieked in the water, showing the gap between her teeth, as – it crossed his mind – she must do when among her own people. Occasionally he had to go out to dinner at the houses of colleagues from the mining company; she sewed and listened to the radio in the flat and he found her in the bed, warm and already asleep, by the time he came in. He made his way into her body without speaking; she made him welcome without a word. Once he put on evening dress for a dinner at his country's consulate; watching him brush one or two fallen hairs from the shoulders of the dark jacket that sat so well on him, she saw a huge room, all chandeliers and people dancing some dance from a costume film – stately, hand-to-hand. She supposed he was going to fetch, in her place in the car, a partner for the evening. They never kissed when either left the flat; he said, suddenly, kindly, pausing as he picked up cigarettes and keys, 'Don't be lonely.' And added, 'Wouldn't you like to visit your family sometimes, when I have to go out?'

He had told her he was going home to his mother in the forests and mountains of his country near the Italian border (he showed her on the map) after Christmas. She had not told him how her mother, not knowing there was any other variety, assumed he was a medical doctor, so she had talked to her about the doctor's children and the doctor's wife who was a very kind lady, glad to have someone who could help out in the surgery as well as the flat.

She remarked wonderingly on his ability to work until midnight or later, after a day at work. She was so tired when she came home from her cash register at the supermarket that once dinner was eaten she could scarcely keep awake. He explained in a way she could understand that while the work she did was repetitive, undemanding of any real response from her intelligence, requiring little mental or physical effort and therefore unrewarding, his work was his greatest interest, it taxed his mental capacities to their limit, exercised all his concentration, and rewarded him constantly as much with the excitement of a problem presented as with the satisfaction of a problem solved. He said later, putting away his papers, speaking out of a silence: 'Have you done other kinds of work?' She said, 'I was in a clothing factory before. Sportbeau shirts; you know? But the pay's better in the shop.'

Of course. Being a conscientious newspaper-reader in every country he lived in, he was aware that it was only recently that the retail consumer trade in this one had been allowed to employ coloureds as shop assistants; even punching a cash register represented advancement. With the continuing shortage of semi-skilled whites a girl like this might be able to edge a little farther into the white-collar category. He began to teach her to type. He was aware that her English was poor, even though, as a foreigner, in his ears her pronunciation did not offend, nor categorize her as it would in those of someone of his education whose mother tongue was English. He corrected her grammatical mistakes but missed the less obvious ones because of his own sometimes exotic English usage – she continued to use the singular pronoun 'it' when what was required was the plural 'they'. Because he was a foreigner (although so clever, as she saw) she was less inhibited than she might have been by the words she knew she misspelled in her typing. While she sat at the typewriter she thought how one day she would type notes for him, as well as making coffee the way he liked it, and taking him inside her body without saying anything, and sitting (even if only through the empty streets of quiet Sundays) beside him in his car, like a wife.

On a summer night near Christmas – he had already bought and hidden a slightly showy but nevertheless good watch he thought she would like – there was a knocking at the door that brought her out of the bathroom and him to his feet, at his work-table. No one ever came to the flat at night; he had no friends intimate enough to drop in without warning. The summons was an imperious banging that did not pause and clearly would not stop until the door was opened.

She stood in the open bathroom doorway gazing at him across the passage into the living-room; her bare feet and shoulders were free of a big bath-towel. She said nothing, did not even whisper. The flat seemed to shake with the strong unhurried blows.

He made as if to go to the door, at last, but now she ran and clutched him by both arms. She shook her head wildly; her lips drew back but her teeth were clenched, she didn't speak. She pulled him into the bedroom, snatched some clothes from the clean laundry laid out on the bed and got into the wall-cupboard, thrusting the key at his hand. Although his arms and calves felt weakly cold he was horrified, distastefully embarrassed at the sight of her pressed back crouching there under his suits and coat; it was horrible and ridiculous. *Come out!* he whispered. *No! Come out!* She hissed: *Where? Where can I go?*

Never mind! Get out of there!

He put out his hand to grasp her. At bay, she said with all the force of her terrible whisper, baring the gap in her teeth: *I'll throw myself out the window.*

She forced the key into his hand like the handle of a knife. He closed the door on her face and drove the key home in the lock, then dropped it among coins in his trouser pocket.

He unslotted the chain that was looped across the flat door. He turned the serrated knob of the Yale lock. The three policemen, two in plain clothes, stood there without impatience although they had been banging on the door for several minutes. The big dark one with an elaborate moustache held out in a hand wearing a plaited gilt ring some sort of identity card.

Dr von Leinsdorf said quietly, the blood coming strangely back to legs and arms, 'What is it?'

The sergeant told him they knew there was a coloured girl in the flat. They had had information; 'I been watching this flat three months, I know.'

'I am alone here.' Dr von Leinsdorf did not raise his voice.

'I know, I know who is here. Come –' And the sergeant and his two assistants went into the living-room, the kitchen, the bathroom (the sergeant picked up a bottle of after-shave cologne, seemed to study the French label) and the bedroom. The assistants removed the clean laundry that was laid upon the bed and then turned back the bedding, carrying the sheets over to be examined by the sergeant under the lamp. They talked to one another in Afrikaans, which the Doctor did not understand. The sergeant himself looked under the bed, and lifted the long curtains at the window. The wall cupboard was of the kind that has no knobs; he saw that it was locked and began to ask in Afrikaans, then politely changed to English, 'Give us the key.'

Dr von Leinsdorf said, 'I'm sorry, I left it at my office – I always lock and take my keys with me in the mornings.'

'It's no good, man, you better give me the key.'

He smiled a little, reasonably. 'It's on my office desk.'

The assistants produced a screwdriver and he watched while they inserted it where the cupboard doors met, gave it quick, firm but not forceful leverage. He heard the lock give.

She had been naked, it was true, when they knocked. But now she was wearing a long-sleeved T-shirt with an appliquéd butterfly motif on one breast, and a pair of jeans. Her feet were still bare; she had managed, by feel, in the dark, to get into some of the clothing she had snatched from the bed, but she had no shoes. She had perhaps been weeping behind the cupboard door (her cheeks looked stained) but now her face was sullen and she was breathing heavily, her diaphragm contracting and expanding exaggeratedly and her breasts pushing against the cloth. It made her appear angry; it might simply have been that she was half-suffocated in the cupboard and needed oxygen. She did not look at Dr von Leinsdorf. She would not reply to the sergeant's questions.

They were taken to the police station where they were at

once separated and in turn led for examination by the district surgeon. The man's underwear was taken away and examined, as the sheets had been, for signs of his seed. When the girl was undressed, it was discovered that beneath her jeans she was wearing a pair of men's briefs with his name on the neatly-sewn laundry tag; in her haste, she had taken the wrong garment to her hiding-place.

Now she cried, standing there before the district surgeon in a man's underwear.

He courteously pretended not to notice. He handed briefs, jeans and T-shirt round the door, and motioned her to lie on a white-sheeted high table where he placed her legs apart, resting in stirrups, and put into her where the other had made his way so warmly a cold hard instrument that expanded wider and wider. Her thighs and knees trembled uncontrollably while the doctor looked into her and touched her deep inside with more hard instruments, carrying wafers of gauze.

When she came out of the examining room back to the charge office, Dr von Leinsdorf was not there; they must have taken him somewhere else. She spent what was left of the night in a cell, as he must be doing; but early in the morning she was released and taken home to her mother's house in the coloured township by a white man who explained he was the clerk of the lawyer who had been engaged for her by Dr von Leinsdorf. Dr von Leinsdorf, the clerk said, had also been bailed out that morning. He did not say when, or if she would see him again.

A statement made by the girl to the police was handed in to Court when she and the man appeared to meet charges of contravening the Immorality Act in a Johannesburg flat on the night of — December, 19—. 'I lived with the white man in his flat. He had intercourse with me sometimes. He gave me tablets to take to prevent me becoming pregnant.'

Interviewed by the Sunday papers, the girl said, 'I'm sorry for the sadness brought to my mother.' She said she was one of nine children of a female laundry worker. She had left school in Standard Three because there was no money at home for gym clothes or a school blazer. She had worked as a machinist in a factory and a cashier in a supermarket. Dr von Leinsdorf taught her to type his notes.

Dr Franz-Josef von Leinsdorf, described as the grandson of a baroness, a cultured man engaged in international mineralogical research, said he accepted social distinctions between people but didn't think they should be legally imposed. 'Even in my own country it's difficult for a person from a higher class to marry one from a lower class.'

The two accused gave no evidence. They did not greet or speak to each other in Court. The Defence argued that the sergeant's evidence that they had been living together as man and wife was hearsay. (The woman with the dachshund, the caretaker?) The magistrate acquitted them because the State failed to prove carnal intercourse had taken place on the night of — December, 19—.

The girl's mother was quoted, with photograph, in the Sunday papers: 'I won't let my daughter work as a servant for a white man again.'

Country Lovers

The farm children play together when they are small; but once the white children go away to school they soon don't play together any more, even in the holidays. Although most of the black children get some sort of schooling, they drop every year farther behind the grades passed by the white children; the childish vocabulary, the child's exploration of the adventurous possibilities of dam, koppies, mealie lands and veld – there comes a time when the white children have surpassed these with the vocabulary of boarding-school and the possibilities of inter-school sports matches and the kind of adventures seen at the cinema. This usefully coincides with the age of twelve or thirteen; so that by the time early adolescence is reached, the black children are making, along with the bodily changes common to all, an easy transition to adult forms of address, beginning to call their old playmates *missus* and *baasie* – little master.

The trouble was Paulus Eysendyck did not seem to realize that Thebedi was now simply one of the crowd of farm children down at the kraal, recognizable in his sisters' old clothes. The first Christmas holidays after he had gone to boarding-school he brought home for Thebedi a painted box he had made in his wood-work class. He had to give it to her secretly because he had nothing for the other children at the kraal. And she gave him, before he went back to school, a bracelet she had made of thin brass wire and the grey-and-white beans of the castor-oil crop his father cultivated. (When they used to play together, she was the one who had taught Paulus how to make clay oxen for their toy spans.) There was a craze, even in the *platteland* towns like the one where he was at school, for boys to wear elephant-hair and other bracelets beside their watch-straps; his was admired, friends asked him to get similar ones for them. He said the natives made them on his father's farm and he would try.

When he was fifteen, six feet tall, and tramping round at school dances with the girls from the 'sister' school in the same town; when he had learnt how to tease and flirt and fondle quite intimately these girls who were the daughters of prosperous farmers like his father; when he had even met one who, at a wedding he had attended with his parents on a nearby farm, had let him do with her in a locked storeroom what people did when they made love – when he was as far from his childhood as all this, he still brought home from a shop in town a red plastic belt and gilt hoop ear-rings for the black girl, Thebedi. She told her father the missus had given these to her as a reward for some work she had done – it was true she sometimes was called to help out in the farmhouse. She told the girls in the kraal that she had a sweetheart nobody knew about, far away, away on another farm, and they giggled, and teased, and admired her. There was a boy in the kraal called Njabulo who said he wished he could have bought her a belt and ear-rings.

When the farmer's son was home for the holidays she wandered far from the kraal and her companions. He went for walks alone. They had not arranged this; it was an urge each followed independently. He knew it was she, from a long way off. She knew that his dog would not bark at her. Down at the dried-up river-bed where five or six years ago the children had caught a leguaan one great day – a creature that combined ideally the size and ferocious aspect of the crocodile with the harmlessness of the lizard – they squatted side by side on the earth bank. He told her traveller's tales: about school, about the punishments at school, particularly, exaggerating both their nature and his indifference to them. He told her about the town of Middleburg, which she had never seen. She had nothing to tell but she prompted with many questions, like any good listener. While he talked he twisted and tugged at the roots of white stinkwood and Cape willow trees that looped out of the eroded earth around them. It had always been a good spot for children's games, down there hidden by the mesh of old, ant-eaten trees held in place by vigorous ones, wild asparagus bushing up between the trunks, and here and there prickly-pear cactus sunken-skinned and bristly, like an old man's face, keeping alive sapless until the next rainy season. She punctured the dry hide of a prickly-pear again and again with a sharp stick while she listened. She laughed a lot at what he told her, sometimes dropping her face on her knees, sharing amusement with the cool shady earth beneath her bare feet. She put on her pair of shoes – white sandals, thickly Blanco-ed against the farm dust – when he was on the farm, but these were taken off and laid aside, at the river-bed.

One summer afternoon when there was water flowing there and it was very hot she waded in as they used to do when they were children, her dress bunched modestly and tucked into the legs of her pants. The schoolgirls he went swimming with at dams or pools on neighbouring farms wore bikinis but the sight of their dazzling bellies and thighs in the sunlight had never made him feel what he felt now, when the girl came up the bank and sat beside him, the drops of water beading off her dark legs the only points of light in the earth-smelling, deep shade. They were not afraid of one another, they had known one another always; he did with her what he had done that time in the storeroom at the wedding, and this time it was so lovely, so lovely, he was surprised . . . and she was surprised by it, too – he could see in her dark face that was part of the shade, with her big dark eyes, shiny as soft water, watching him attentively: as she had when they used to huddle over their teams of mud oxen, as she had when he told her about detention weekends at school.

They went to the river-bed often through those summer holidays. They met just before the light went, as it does quite quickly, and each returned home with the dark – she to her mother's hut, he to the farmhouse – in time for the evening meal. He did not tell her about school or town any more. She did not ask questions any longer. He told her, each time, when they would meet again. Once or twice it was very early in the morning; the lowing of the cows being driven to graze came to them where they lay, dividing them with unspoken recognition of the sound read in their two pairs of eyes, opening so close to each other.

He was a popular boy at school. He was in the second, then the first soccer team. The head girl of the 'sister' school was said to have a crush on him; he didn't particularly like her, but there was a pretty blonde who put up her long hair into a kind of doughnut with a black ribbon round it, whom he took to see films when the schoolboys and girls had a free Saturday afternoon. He had been driving tractors and other farm vehicles since he was ten years old, and as soon as he was eighteen he got a driver's licence and in the holidays, this last year of his school-life, he took neighbours' daughters to dances and to the drive-in cinema that had just opened twenty kilometres from the farm. His sisters were married, by then; his parents often left him in charge of the farm over the weekend while they visited the young wives and grandchildren.

When Thebedi saw the farmer and his wife drive away on a Saturday afternoon, the boot of their Mercedes filled with fresh-killed poultry and vegetables from the garden that it was part of her father's work to tend, she knew that she must come not to the river-bed but up to the house. The house was an old one, thick-walled, dark against the heat. The kitchen was its lively thoroughfare, with servants, food supplies, begging cats and dogs, pots boiling over, washing being damped for ironing, and the big deep-freeze the missus had ordered from town, bearing a crocheted mat and a vase of plastic irises. But the dining-room with the bulging-legged heavy table was shut up in its rich, old smell of soup and tomato sauce. The sitting-room curtains were drawn and the T.V. set silent. The door of the parents' bedroom was locked and the empty rooms where the girls had slept had sheets of plastic spread over the beds. It was in one of these that she and the farmer's son stayed together whole nights – almost: she had to get away before the house servants, who knew her, came in at dawn. There was a risk someone would discover her or traces of her presence if he took her to his own bedroom, although she had looked into it many times when she was helping out in the house and knew well, there, the row of silver cups he had won at school.

When she was eighteen and the farmer's son nineteen and working with his father on the farm before entering a veterinary college, the young man Njabulo asked her father for her. Njabulo's parents met with hers and the money he was to pay in place of the cows it is customary to give a prospective bride's parents was settled upon. He had no cows to offer; he was a labourer on the Eysendyck farm, like her father. A bright youngster; old Eysendyck had taught him bricklaying and was using him for odd jobs in construction, around the place. She did not tell the farmer's son that her parents had arranged for her to marry. She did not tell him, either, before he left for his first term at the veterinary college, that she thought she was going to have a baby. Two months after her marriage to Njabulo, she gave birth to a daughter. There was no disgrace in that; among her people it is customary for a young man to make sure, before marriage, that the chosen girl is not barren, and Njabulo had made love to her then. But the infant was very light and did not quickly grow darker as most African babies do. Already at birth there was on its head a quantity of straight, fine floss, like that which carries the seeds of certain weeds in the veld. The unfocused eyes it opened were grey flecked with yellow. Njabulo was the matt, opaque coffee-grounds colour that has always been called black; the colour of Thebedi's legs on which beaded water looked oyster-shell blue, the same colour as Thebedi's face, where the black eyes, with their interested gaze and clear whites, were so dominant.

Njabulo made no complaint. Out of his farm labourer's earnings he bought from the Indian store a cellophane-windowed pack containing a pink plastic bath, six napkins, a card of safety pins, a knitted jacket, cap and bootees, a dress, and a tin of Johnson's Baby Powder, for Thebedi's baby.

When it was two weeks old Paulus Eysendyck arrived home from the veterinary college for the holidays. He drank a glass of fresh, still-warm milk in the childhood familiarity of his mother's kitchen and heard her discussing with the old house-servant where they could get a reliable substitute to help out now that the girl Thebedi had had a baby. For the first time since he was a small boy he came right into the kraal. It was eleven o'clock in the morning. The men were at work in the lands. He looked about him, urgently; the women turned away, each not wanting to be the one approached to point out where Thebedi lived. Thebedi appeared, coming slowly from the hut Njabulo had built in white man's style, with a tin chimney, and a proper window with glass panes set in straight as walls made of unfired bricks would allow. She greeted him with hands brought together and a token movement representing the respectful bob with which she was accustomed to acknowledge she was in the presence of his father or mother. He lowered his head under the doorway of her home and went in. He said, 'I want to see. Show me.'

She had taken the bundle off her back before she came out

into the light to face him. She moved between the iron bedstead made up with Njabulo's checked blankets and the small wooden table where the pink plastic bath stood among food and kitchen pots, and picked up the bundle from the snugly blanketed grocer's box where it lay. The infant was asleep; she revealed the closed, pale, plump tiny face, with a bubble of spit at the corner of the mouth, the spidery pink hands stirring. She took off the woollen cap and the straight fine hair flew up after it in static electricity, showing gilded strands here and there. He said nothing. She was watching him as she had done when they were little, and the gang of children had trodden down a crop in their games or transgressed in some other way for which he, as the farmer's son, the white one among them, must intercede with the farmer. She disturbed the sleeping face by scratching or tickling gently at a cheek with one finger, and slowly the eyes opened, saw nothing, were still asleep, and then, awake, no longer narrowed, looked out at them, grey with yellowish flecks, his own hazel eyes.

He struggled for a moment with a grimace of tears, anger and self-pity. She could not put out her hand to him. He said, 'You haven't been near the house with it?'

She shook her head.

'Never?'

Again she shook her head.

'Don't take it out. Stay inside. Can't you take it away somewhere. You must give it to someone –'

She moved to the door with him.

He said, 'I'll see what I will do. I don't know.' And then he said: 'I feel like killing myself.'

Her eyes began to glow, to thicken with tears. For a moment there was the feeling between them that used to come when they were alone down at the river-bed.

He walked out.

Two days later, when his mother and father had left the

farm for the day, he appeared again. The women were away on the lands, weeding, as they were employed to do as casual labour in summer; only the very old remained, propped up on the ground outside the huts in the flies and the sun. Thebedi did not ask him in. The child had not been well; it had diarrhoea. He asked where its food was. She said, 'The milk comes from me.' He went into Njabulo's house, where the child lay; she did not follow but stayed outside the door and watched without seeing an old crone who had lost her mind, talking to herself, talking to the fowls who ignored her.

She thought she heard small grunts from the hut, the kind of infant grunt that indicates a full stomach, a deep sleep. After a time, long or short she did not know, he came out and walked away with plodding stride (his father's gait) out of sight, towards his father's house.

The baby was not fed during the night and although she kept telling Njabulo it was sleeping, he saw for himself in the morning that it was dead. He comforted her with words and caresses. She did not cry but simply sat, staring at the door. Her hands were cold as dead chickens' feet to his touch.

Njabulo buried the little baby where farm workers were buried, in the place in the veld the farmer had given them. Some of the mounds had been left to weather away unmarked, others were covered with stones and a few had fallen wooden crosses. He was going to make a cross but before it was finished the police came and dug up the grave and took away the dead baby: someone – one of the other labourers? their women? – had reported that the baby was almost white, that, strong and healthy, it had died suddenly after a visit by the farmer's son. Pathological tests on the infant corpse showed intestinal damage not always consistent with death by natural causes.

Thebedi went for the first time to the country town where

Paulus had been to school, to give evidence at the preparatory examination into the charge of murder brought against him. She cried hysterically in the witness box, saying yes, yes (the gilt hoop ear-rings swung in her ears), she saw the accused pouring liquid into the baby's mouth. She said he had threatened to shoot her if she told anyone.

More than a year went by before, in that same town, the case was brought to trial. She came to Court with a new-born baby on her back. She wore gilt hoop ear-rings; she was calm; she said she had not seen what the white man did in the house.

Paulus Eysendyck said he had visited the hut but had not poisoned the child.

The Defence did not contest that there had been a love relationship between the accused and the girl, or that intercourse had taken place, but submitted there was no proof that the child was the accused's.

The judge told the accused there was strong suspicion against him but not enough proof that he had committed the crime. The Court could not accept the girl's evidence because it was clear she had committed perjury either at this trial or at the preparatory examination. There was the suggestion in the mind of the Court that she might be an accomplice in the crime; but, again insufficient proof.

The judge commended the honourable behaviour of the husband (sitting in court in a brown-and-yellow-quartered golf cap bought for Sundays) who had not rejected his wife and had 'even provided clothes for the unfortunate infant out of his slender means'.

The verdict on the accused was 'not guilty'.

The young white man refused to accept the congratulations of press and public and left the Court with his mother's raincoat shielding his face from photographers. His father said to the press, 'I will try and carry on as best I can to hold up my head in the district.'

Interviewed by the Sunday papers, who spelled her name in a variety of ways, the black girl, speaking in her own language, was quoted beneath her photograph: 'It was a thing of our childhood, we don't see each other any more.'

Not For Publication

It is not generally known – and it is never mentioned in the official biographies – that the Prime Minister spent the first eleven years of his life, as soon as he could be trusted not to get under a car, leading his uncle about the streets. His uncle was not really blind, but nearly, and he was certainly mad. He walked with his right hand on the boy's left shoulder; they kept moving part of the day, but they also had a pitch on the cold side of the street, between the legless man near the post office who sold bootlaces and copper bracelets, and the one with the doll's hand growing out of one elbow, whose pitch was outside the Y.W.C.A. That was where Adelaide Graham-Grigg found the boy, and later he explained to her, 'If you sit in the sun they don't give you anything.'

Miss Graham-Grigg was not looking for Praise Basetse. She was in Johannesburg on one of her visits from a British Protectorate, seeing friends, pulling strings and pursuing, on the side, her private study of following up the fate of those people of the tribe who had crossed the border and lost themselves, sometimes over several generations, in the city. As she felt down through the papers and letters in her bag to find a sixpence for the old man's hat, she heard him mumble something to the boy in the tribe's tongue – which was not in itself anything very significant in this city where many African languages could be heard. But these sounds formed in her ear as words: it was the language that she had learnt to understand a little. She asked, in English, using only the traditional form of address in the tribe's tongue, whether the old man was a tribesman. But he was mumbling the blessings that the clink of a coin started up like a kick to a worn and useless mechanism. The boy spoke to him, nudged him; he had already learnt in a rough way to be a businessman. Then the old man protested, no, no, he had come a long time from that tribe. A long, long time. He was Johannesburg. She saw that he confused the question with some routine interrogation at the pass offices, where a man from another territory was always in danger of being endorsed out to some forgotten 'home'. She spoke to the boy, asking him if he came from the Protectorate. He shook his head terrifiedly; once before he had been ordered off the streets by a welfare organization. 'But your father? Your mother?' Miss Graham-Grigg said, smiling. She discovered that the old man had come from the Protectorate, from the very village she had made her own, and that his children and grandchildren continued to speak the language as their mother tongue, among themselves, down to the second generation born in the alien city.

Now the pair were no longer beggars to be ousted from her conscience by a coin: they were members of the tribe. She found out what township they went to ground in after the day's begging, interviewed the family, established for them the old man's right to a pension in his adopted country, and above all, did something for the boy. She never succeeded in finding out exactly who he was – she gathered he must have been the illegitimate child of one of the girls of the family, his parentage concealed so that she might go on with her schooling. Anyway, he was a descendant of the tribe, a displaced tribesman, and he could not be left to go on begging in the streets.

That was as far as Miss Graham-Grigg's thoughts for him went, in the beginning. Nobody wanted him particularly, and she met with no opposition from the family when she proposed to take him back to the Protectorate and put him to school. He went with her just as he had gone through the streets of Johannesburg each day under the weight of the old man's hand.

The boy had never been to school before. He could not write, but Miss Graham-Grigg was astonished to discover that he could read quite fluently. Sitting beside her in her little car in the khaki shorts and shirt she had bought him, stripped of the protection of his smelly rags and scrubbed bare to her questions, he told her that he had learnt from the newspaper vender whose pitch was on the corner: from the posters that changed several times a day, and then from the front pages of the newspapers and magazines spread there. Good God, what had he not learnt on the street! Everything from his skin out unfamiliar to him, and even that smelling strangely different – this detachment, she realized, made the child talk as he could never have done when he was himself. Without differentiation, he related the commonplaces of his life; he had also learnt from the legless, copper-bracelet man how to make *dagga* cigarettes and smoke them for a nice feeling. She asked him what he thought he would have done when he got older, if he had had to keep on walking with his uncle, and he said that he had wanted to belong to one of the gangs of boys, some little older than himself, who were very good at making money. They got money from white people's pockets and handbags without their even knowing it, and if the police came they began to play penny whistles and sing. She said with a smile, 'Well, you can forget all about the street, now. You don't have to think about it ever again.' And he said, 'Yes, med-dam,' and she knew she had no idea what he was thinking – how could she? All she could offer were more unfamiliarities, the unfamiliarities of generalized encouragement, saying, 'And soon you will know how to write.'

She had noticed that he was hatefully ashamed of not being able to write. When he had had to admit it, the face that he turned open and victimized to her every time she spoke had the squinting grimace – teeth showing and a grown-up cut between the faint, child's eyebrows – of profound humiliation. Humiliation terrified Adelaide Graham-Grigg as the spectacle of savage anger terrifies others. That was one of the things she held against the missionaries: how they stressed Christ's submission to humiliation, and so had conditioned the people of Africa to humiliation by the white man.

Praise went to the secular school that Miss Graham-Grigg's committee of friends of the tribe in London had helped pay to set up in the village in opposition to the mission school. The sole qualified teacher was a young man who had received his training in South Africa and now had been brought back to serve his people; but it was a beginning. As Adelaide Graham-Grigg often said to the Chief, shining-eyed as any proud daughter, 'By the time independence comes we'll be free not only of the British government, but of the church as well.' And he always giggled a little embarrassedly, although he knew her so well and was old enough to be her father, because her own father was both a former British M.P. and the son of a bishop.

It was true that everything was a beginning; that was the beauty of it – of the smooth mud houses, red earth, flies and heat that visitors from England wondered she could bear to live with for months on end – while their palaces and cathedrals and streets, choked on a thousand years of used-up endeavour, were an ending. Even Praise was a beginning; one day the tribe would be economically strong enough to gather its exiles home, and it would no longer be necessary for its sons to sell their labour over that border. But it soon became clear that Praise was also exceptional. The business of learning to read from newspaper headlines was not merely a piece of gutter wit; it proved to have been the irrepressible urge of real intelligence. In six weeks the boy could write, and from the start he could spell perfectly, while boys of sixteen and eighteen never succeeded in mastering English orthography. His arithmetic was so good that he had to be taught with the Standard Three class instead of the beginners; he grasped at once what a map was; and in his spare time showed a remarkable aptitude for understanding the workings of various mechanisms, from water-pumps to motor-cycle engines. In eighteen months he had completed the Standard Five syllabus, only a year behind the average age of a city white child with all the background advantage of a literate home.

There was as yet no other child in the tribe's school who was ready for Standard Six. It was difficult to see what could be done, now, but send Praise back over the border to school. So Miss Graham-Grigg decided it would have to be Father Audry. There was nothing else for it. The only alternative was the mission school, those damned Jesuits who'd been sitting in the Protectorate since the days when the white imperialists were on the grab, taking the tribes under their 'protection' – and the children the boy would be in class with there wouldn't provide any sort of stimulation, either. So it would have to be Father Audry, and South Africa. He was a priest, too, an Anglican one, but his school was a place where at least, along with the pious pap, a black child could get an education as good as a white child's.

When Praise came out into the veld with the other boys his eyes screwed up against the size: the land ran away all round, and there was no other side to be seen; only the sudden appearance of the sky, that was even bigger. The wind made him snuff like a dog. He stood helpless as the country men he had seen caught by changing traffic lights in the middle of a street. The bits of space between buildings came together, ballooned uninterruptedly over him, he was lost; but there were clouds as big as the buildings had been, and even though space was vaster than any city, it was peopled by birds. If you ran for ten minutes into the veld the village was gone; but down low on the ground thousands of ants knew their way between their hard mounds that stood up endlessly as the land.

He went to herd cattle with the other boys early in the mornings and after school. He taught them some gambling games they had never heard of. He told them about the city they had never seen. The money in the old man's hat seemed a lot to them, who had never got more than a few pennies when the mail train stopped for water at the halt five miles away; so the sum grew in his own estimation too, and he exaggerated it a bit. In any case, he *was* forgetting about the city, in a way; not Miss Graham-Grigg's way, but in the manner of a child, who makes, like a wasp building with its own spittle, his private context within the circumstances of his surroundings, so that the space around him was reduced to the village, the pan where the cattle were taken to drink, the halt where the train went by; whatever particular patch of sand or rough grass astir with ants the boys rolled on, heads together, among the white egrets and the cattle. He learnt from the others what roots and leaves were good to chew, and how to set wire traps for spring-hares. Though Miss Graham-Grigg had said he need not, he went to church with the children on Sundays.

He did not live where she did, in one of the Chief 's houses, but with the family of one of the other boys; but he was at her house often. She asked him to copy letters for her. She cut things out of the newspapers she got and gave them to him to read; they were about aeroplanes, and dams being built, and the way the people lived in other countries. 'Now you'll be able to tell the boys all about the Volta Dam, that is also in Africa – far from here – but still, in Africa,' she said, with that sudden smile that reddened her face. She had a gramophone and she played records for him. Not only music, but people reading our poems, so that he knew that the poems in the school reader were not just short lines of words, but more like songs. She gave him tea with plenty of sugar and she asked him to help her to learn the language of the tribe, to talk to her in it. He was not allowed to call her *madam* or *missus*, as he did the white women who had put money in the hat, but had to learn to say *Miss Graham-Grigg.*

Although he had never known any white women before except as high-heeled shoes passing quickly in the street, he did not think that all white women must be like her; in the light of what he had seen white people, in their cars, their wealth, their distance, to be, he understood nothing that she did. She looked like them, with her blue eyes, blonde hair and skin that was not one colour but many; brown where the sun burned it, red when she blushed – but she lived here in the Chief's houses, drove him in his car, and sometimes slept out in the fields with the women when they were harvesting kaffircorn far from the village. He did not know why she had brought him there or why she should be kind to him. But he could not ask her, any more than he would have asked her why she went out and slept in the fields when she had a gramophone and a lovely gas lamp (he had been able to repair it for her) in her room. If, when they were talking together, the talk came anywhere near the pitch outside the post office, she became slowly very red, and they went past it, either by falling silent or (on her part) talking and laughing rather fast.

That was why he was amazed the day she told him that he was going back to Johannesburg. As soon as she had said it she blushed darkly for it, her eyes pleading confusion: so it was really from her that the vision of the pitch outside the post office came again. But she was already speaking: '. . . to school. To a really good boarding-school. Father Audry's school, about nine miles from town. You must get your chance at a good school, Praise. We really can't teach you properly any longer. Maybe you'll be the teacher here yourself, one day. There'll be a high school, and you'll be the headmaster.'

She succeeded in making him smile, but she looked sad, uncertain. He went on smiling because he couldn't tell her about the initiation school that he was about to begin with the other boys of his age-group. Perhaps someone would tell her. The other women. Even the Chief. But you couldn't fool her with smiling.

'You'll be sorry to leave Tebedi and Joseph and the rest.'

He stood there, smiling.

'Praise, I don't think you understand about yourself – about your brain.' She gave a little sobbing giggle, prodded at her own head. 'You've got an awfully good one. More in there than other boys – you know? It's something special – it would be such a waste. Lots of people would like to be clever like you, but it's not easy, when you are the clever one.'

He went on smiling. He did not want her face looking into his any more and so he fixed his eyes on her feet, white feet in sandals with the veins standing out over the ankles like the feet of Christ dangling above his head in the church.

Adelaide Graham-Grigg had met Father Audry before, of course. All those white people who do not accept the colour bar in southern Africa seem to know each other, however different the bases of their rejection. She had sat with him on some committee or other in London a few years earlier, along with a couple of exiled white South African leftists and a black nationalist leader. Anyway, everyone knew him – from the newspapers, if nowhere else: he had been warned, in a public speech by the Prime Minister of the South African Republic, Dr Verwoerd, that the interference of a churchman in political matters would not be tolerated. He continued to speak his mind, and (as the newspapers quoted him) 'to obey the commands of God before the dictates of the State'. He had close friends among African and Indian leaders, and it was said that he even got on well with certain ministers of the Dutch Reformed Church, that, in fact, *he* was behind some of the dissidents who now and then questioned Divine Sanction for the colour bar – such was the presence of his restless, black-cassocked figure, stammering eloquence, and jagged handsome face.

He had aged since she saw him last; he was less handsome. But he had still what he would have as long as he lived: the unconscious bearing of a natural prince among men that makes a celebrated actor, a political leader, a successful lover; an object of attraction and envy who, whatever his generosity of spirit, is careless of one cruelty for which other people will never forgive him – the distinction, the luck with which he was born.

He was tired and closed his eyes in a grimace straining at concentration when he talked to her, yet in spite of this, she felt the dimness of the candle of her being within his radius. Everything was right with him; nothing was quite right with her. She was only thirty-six but she had never looked any younger. Her eyes were the bright shy eyes of a young woman, but her feet and hands with their ridged nails had the look of tension and suffering of extremities that would never caress: she saw it, she saw it, she knew in his presence that they were deprived for ever.

Her humiliation gave her force. She said, 'I must tell you we want him back in the tribe – I mean, there are terribly few with enough education even for administration. Within the next few years we'll desperately need more and more educated men . . . We shouldn't want him to be allowed to think of becoming a priest.'

Father Audry smiled at what he knew he was expected to come out with: that if the boy chose the way of the Lord, etc.

He said, 'What you want is someone who will turn out to be an able politician without challenging the tribal system.'

They both laughed, but, again, he had unconsciously taken the advantage of admitting their deeply divergent views; he believed the chiefs must go, while she, of course, saw no reason why Africans shouldn't develop their own tribal democracy instead of taking over the Western pattern.

'Well, he's a little young for us to be worrying about that now, don't you think?' He smiled. There were a great many papers on his desk, and she had the sense of pressure of his preoccupation with other things. 'What about the Lemeribe Mission? What's the teaching like these days – I used to know Father Chalmon when he was there –'

'I wouldn't send him to those people,' she said spiritedly, implying that he knew her views on missionaries and their role in Africa. In this atmosphere of candour, they discussed Praise's background. Father Audry suggested that the boy should be encouraged to resume relations with his family, once he was back within reach of Johannesburg.

'They're pretty awful.'

'It would be best for him to acknowledge what he was, if he is to accept what he is to become.' He got up with a swish of his black skirts and strode, stooping in the opened door, to call, 'Simon, bring the boy.' Miss Graham-Grigg was smiling excitedly towards the doorway, all the will to love pacing behind the bars of her glance.

Praise entered in the navy-blue shorts and white shirt of his new school uniform. The woman's kindness, the man's attention, got him in the eyes like the sun striking off the pan where the cattle had been taken to drink. Father Audry came from England, Miss Graham-Grigg had told him, like herself. That was what they were, these two white people who were not like any white people he had seen to be. What they were was being English. From far off; six thousand miles from here, as he knew from his geography book.

*

Praise did very well at the new school. He sang in the choir in the big church on Sundays; his body, that was to have been made a man's out in the bush, was hidden under the white robes. The boys smoked in the lavatories and once there was a girl who came and lay down for them in a storm-water ditch behind the workshops. He knew all about these things from before, on the streets and in the location where he had slept in one room with a whole family. But he did not tell the boys about the initiation. The women had not said anything to Miss Graham-Grigg. The Chief hadn't, either. Soon when Praise thought about it he realized that by now it must be over. Those boys must have come back from the bush. Miss Graham-Grigg had said that after a year, when Christmas came, she would fetch him for the summer holidays. She did come and see him twice that first year, when she was down in Johannesburg, but he couldn't go back with her at Christmas because Father Audry had him in the Nativity play and was giving him personal coaching in Latin and algebra. Father Audry didn't actually teach in the school at all – it was 'his' school simply because he had begun it, and it was run by the order of which he was Father Provincial – but the reports of the boy's progress were so astonishing that, as he said to Miss Graham-Grigg, one felt one must give him all the mental stimulation one could.

'I begin to believe we may be able to sit him for his matric when he is just sixteen.' Father Audry made the pronouncement with the air of doing so at the risk of sounding ridiculous. Miss Graham-Grigg always had her hair done when she got to Johannesburg, she was looking pretty and gay. 'D'you think he could do a Cambridge entrance? My committee in London would set up a scholarship, I'm sure – investment in a future prime minister for the Protectorate!'

When Praise was sent for, she said she hardly knew him; he hadn't grown much, but he looked so *grown-up*, with his long trousers and glasses. 'You really needn't wear them when you're not working,' said Father Audry. 'Well, I suppose if you take 'em on and off you keep leaving them about, eh?' They both stood back, smiling, letting the phenomenon embody in the boy.

Praise saw that she had never been reminded by anyone about the initiation. She began to give him news of his friends, Tebedi and Joseph and the others, but when he heard their names they seemed to belong to people he couldn't see in his mind.

Father Audry talked to him sometimes about what Father called his 'family', and when first he came to the school he had been told to write to them. It was a well-written, well-spelled letter in English, exactly the letter he presented as a school exercise when one was required in class. They didn't answer. Then Father Audry must have made private efforts to get in touch with them, because the old woman, a couple of children who had been babies when he left and one of his grown-up 'sisters' came to the school on a visiting day. They had to be pointed out to him among the other boys' visitors; he would not have known them, nor they him. He said, 'Where's my uncle?' – because he would have known him at once; he had never grown out of the slight stoop of the left shoulder where the weight of the old man's hand had impressed the young bone. But the old man was dead. Father Audry came up and put a long arm round the bent shoulder and another long arm round one of the small children and said from one to the other, 'Are you going to work hard and learn a lot like your brother?' And the small black child stared up into the nostrils filled with strong hair, the tufted eyebrows, the red mouth surrounded by the pale jowl dark-pored with beard beneath the skin, and then down, torn by fascination, to the string of beads that hung from the leather belt.

They did not come again but Praise did not much miss visitors because he spent more and more time with Father

Audry. When he was not actually being coached, he was set to work to prepare his lessons or do his reading in the Father's study, where he could concentrate as one could not hope to do up at the school. Father Audry taught him chess as a form of mental gymnastics, and was jubilant the first time Praise beat him. Praise went up to the house for a game nearly every evening after supper. He tried to teach the other boys, but after the first ten minutes of explanation of moves, someone would bring out the cards or dice and they would all play one of the old games that were played in the streets and yards and locations. Johannesburg was only nine miles away; you could see the lights.

Father Audry rediscovered what Miss Graham-Grigg had found – that Praise listened attentively to music, serious music. One day Father Audry handed the boy the flute that had lain for years in its velvet-lined box that bore still the little silver name-plate: Rowland Audry. He watched while Praise gave the preliminary swaying wriggle and assumed the bent-kneed stance of all the urchin performers Father Audry had seen, and then tried to blow down it in the shy, fierce attack of penny-whistle music. Father Audry took it out of his hands. 'It's what you've just heard there.' Bach's unaccompanied flute sonata lay on the record-player. Praise smiled and frowned, giving his glasses a lift with his nose – a habit he was developing. 'But you'll soon learn to play it the right way round,' said Father Audry, and with the lack of self-consciousness that comes from the habit of privilege, put the flute to his mouth and played what he remembered after ten years.

He taught Praise not only how to play the flute but also the elements of musical composition, so that he should not simply play by ear, or simply listen with pleasure, but also understand what it was that he heard. The flute-playing was much more of a success with the boys than the chess had been, and on Saturday nights, when they sometimes made up concerts, he was allowed to take it to the hostel and play it for them. Once he played in a show for white people, in Johannesburg; but the boys could not come to that; he could only tell them about the big hall at the university, the jazz band, the African singers and dancers with their red lips and straightened hair, like white women.

The one thing that dissatisfied Father Audry was that the boy had not filled out and grown as much as one would have expected. He made it a rule that Praise must spend more time on physical exercise – the school couldn't afford a proper gymnasium but there was some equipment outdoors. The trouble was that the boy had so little time; even with his exceptional ability, it was not going to be easy for a boy with his lack of background to matriculate at sixteen. Brother George, his form master, was certain he could be made to bring it off; there was a specially strong reason why everyone wanted him to do it since Father Audry had established that he would be eligible for an open scholarship that no black boy had ever won before – what a triumph that would be, for the boy, for the school, for all the African boys who were considered fit only for the inferior standard of 'Bantu education'! Perhaps some day this beggar child from the streets of Johannesburg might even become the first black South African to be a Rhodes Scholar. This was what Father Audry jokingly referred to as Brother George's 'sin of pride'. But who knew? It was not inconceivable. So far as the boy's physique was concerned – what Brother George said was probably true: 'You can't feed up for those years in the streets.'

From the beginning of the first term of the year he was fifteen Praise had to be coached, pressed on, and to work as even he had never worked before. His teachers gave him tremendous support; he seemed borne along on it by either arm so that he never looked up from his books. To encourage him, Father Audry arranged for him to compete in certain inter-school scholastic contests that were really intended for the white Anglican schools – a spelling bee, a debate, a quiz contest. He sat on the platform in the polished halls of huge white schools and gave his correct answers in the African-accented English that the boys who surrounded him knew only as the accent of servants and delivery men.

Brother George often asked him if he were tired. But he was not tired. He only wanted to be left with his books. The boys in the hostel seemed to know this; they never asked him to play cards any more, and even when they shared smokes together in the lavatory, they passed him his drag in silence. He specially did not want Father Audry to come in with a glass of hot milk. He would rest his cheek against the pages of the books, now and then, alone in the study; that was all. The damp stone smell of the books was all he needed. Where he had once had to force himself to return again and again to the pages of things he did not grasp, gazing in blankness at the print until meaning assembled itself, he now had to force himself when it was necessary to leave the swarming facts outside which he no longer seemed to understand anything. Sometimes he could not work for minutes at a time because he was thinking that Father Audry would come in with the milk. When he did come, it was never actually so bad. But Praise couldn't look at his face. Once or twice when he had gone out again, Praise shed a few tears. He found himself praying, smiling with the tears and trembling, rubbing at the scalding water that ran down inside his nose and blotched on the books.

One Saturday afternoon when Father Audry had been entertaining some guests at lunch he came into the study and suggested that the boy should get some fresh air – go out and join the football game for an hour or so. But Praise was struggling with geometry problems from the previous year's matriculation paper that, to Brother George's dismay, he had suddenly got all wrong, that morning.

Father Audry could imagine what Brother George was thinking: was this an example of the phenomenon he had met with so often with African boys of a lesser calibre – the inability, through lack of an assumed cultural background, to perform a piece of work well known to them, once it was presented in a slightly different manner outside one of their own textbooks? Nonsense, of course, in this case; everyone was over-anxious about the boy. Right from the start he'd shown that there was nothing mechanistic about his thought processes; he had a brain, not just a set of conditioned reflexes.

'Off you go. You'll manage better when you've taken a few knocks on the field.'

But desperation had settled on the boy's face like obstinacy. 'I must, I must,' he said, putting his palms down over the books.

'Good. Then let's see if we can tackle it together.'

The black skirt swishing past the shiny shoes brought a smell of cigars. Praise kept his eyes on the black beads; the leather belt they hung from creaked as the big figure sat down. Father Audry took the chair on the opposite side of the table and switched the exercise book round towards himself. He scrubbed at the thick eyebrows till they stood out tangled, drew the hand down over his great nose and then screwed his eyes closed a moment, mouth strangely open and lips drawn back in a familiar grimace. There was a jump, like a single painful hiccup, in Praise's body. The Father was explaining the problem gently, in his offhand English voice.

He said, 'Praise? D'you follow?' – the boy seemed sluggish, almost deaf, as if the voice reached him as the light of a star reaches the earth from something already dead.

Father Audry put out his fine hand, in question or compassion. But the boy leapt up, dodging a blow. 'Sir – no. Sir – no.'

It was clearly hysteria; he had never addressed Father Audry as anything but 'Father'. It was some frightening retrogression, a reversion to the subconscious, a place of symbols and collective memory. He spoke for others, out of another time. Father Audry stood up but saw in alarm that by the boy's retreat he was made his pursuer, and he let him go blundering in clumsy panic out of the room.

Brother George was sent to comfort the boy. In half an hour Praise was down on the football field, running and laughing. But Father Audry took some days to get over the incident. He kept thinking how when the boy had backed away he had almost gone after him. The ugliness of the instinct repelled him; who would have thought how, at the mercy of the instinct to prey, the fox, the wild dog long for the innocence of the gentle rabbit, and the lamb. No one had shown fear of him ever before in his life. He had never given a thought to the people who were not like himself; those from whom others turn away. He felt at last a repugnant and resentful pity for them, the dripping-jawed hunters. He even thought that he would like to go into retreat for a few days, but it was inconvenient – he had so many obligations. Finally, the matter-of-factness of the boy, Praise, was the thing that restored normality. So far as the boy was concerned, one would have thought that nothing had happened. The next day he seemed to have forgotten all about it; a good thing. And so Father Audry's own inner disruption, denied by the boy's calm, sank away. He allowed the whole affair the one acknowledgement of writing to Miss Graham-Grigg – surely that was not making too much of it – to suggest that the boy was feeling the tension of his final great effort, and that a visit from her, etc.; but she was still away in England – some family troubles had kept her there for months, and in fact she had not been to see her protégé for more than a year.

Praise worked steadily on the last lap. Brother George and Father Audry watched him continually. He was doing extremely well and seemed quite overcome with the weight of pride and pleasure when Father Audry presented him with a new black fountain-pen: this was the pen with which he was to write the matriculation exam. On a Monday afternoon Father Audry, who had been in conference with the bishop all morning, looked in on his study, where every afternoon the boy would be seen sitting at the table that had been moved in for him. But there was no one there. The books were on the table. A chute of sunlight landed on the seat of the chair.

Praise was not found again. The school was searched; and then the police were informed; the boys questioned; there were special prayers said in the mornings and evenings. He had not taken anything with him except the fountain-pen.

When everything had been done there was nothing but silence; nobody mentioned the boy's name. But Father Audry was conducting investigations on his own. Every now and then he would get an idea that would bring a sudden hopeful relief. He wrote to Adelaide Graham-Grigg: '. . . what worries me – I believe the boy may have been on the verge of a nervous breakdown. I am hunting everywhere . . .'; was it possible that he might make his way to the Protectorate? She was acting as confidential secretary to the Chief, now, but she wrote to say that if the boy turned up she would try to make time to deal with the situation. Father Audry even sought out, at last, the 'family' – the people with whom Miss Graham-Grigg had discovered Praise living as a beggar. They had been moved to a new township and it took some time to trace them. He found Number 28b, Block E, in the appropriate ethnic group. He was accustomed to going in and out of African homes and he explained his visit to the old woman in matter-of-fact terms at once, since he knew how suspicious of questioning the people would be. There were no interior doors in these houses and a woman in the inner room who was dressing moved out of the visitor's line of vision as he sat down. She heard all that passed between Father Audry and the old woman and presently she came in with mild interest. Out of a silence the old woman was saying, 'My-my-

my-my!' – she shook her head down into her bosom in a stylized expression of commiseration; they had not seen the boy. 'And he spoke so nice, everything was so nice in the school.' But they knew nothing about the boy, nothing at all. The younger woman remarked, 'Maybe he's with those boys who sleep in the old empty cars there in town – you know? – there by the beer hall?'

Oral History

There's always been one house like a white man's house in the village of Dilolo. Built of brick with a roof that bounced signals from the sun. You could see it through the mopane trees as you did the flash of paraffin tins the women carried on their heads, bringing water from the river. The rest of the village was built of river mud, grey, shaped by the hollows of hands, with reed thatch and poles of mopane from which the leaves had been ripped like fish-scales.

It was the chief's house. Some chiefs have a car as well but this was not an important chief, the clan is too small for that, and he had the usual stipend from the government. If they had given him a car he would have had no use for it. There is no road: the army patrol Land Rovers come upon the people's cattle, startled as buck, in the mopane scrub. The village has been there a long time. The chief's grandfather was the clan's grandfathers' chief, and his name is the same as that of the chief who waved his warriors to down assegais and took the first bible from a Scottish Mission Board white man. *Seek and ye shall find*, the missionaries said.

The villagers in those parts don't look up, any more, when the sting-shaped army planes fly over twice a day. Only fish-eagles are disturbed, take off, screaming, keen swerving heads lifting into their invaded domain of sky. The men who have been away to work on the mines can read, but there are no newspapers. The people hear over the radio the government's count of how many army trucks have been blown up, how many white soldiers are going to be buried with *full military honours* – something that is apparently white people's way with their dead.

The chief had a radio, and he could read. He read to the headmen the letter from the government saying that anyone hiding or giving food and water to those who were fighting against the government's army would be put in prison. He read another letter from the government saying that to protect the village from these men who went over the border and came back with guns to kill people and burn huts, anybody who walked in the bush after dark would be shot. Some of the young men who, going courting or drinking to the next village, might have been in danger, were no longer at home in their fathers' care anyway. The young go away: once it was to the mines, now – the radio said – it was over the border to learn how to fight. Sons walked out of the clearing of mud huts; past the chief's house; past the children playing with the models of police patrol Land Rovers made out of twisted wire. The children called out, 'Where are you going?' The young men didn't answer and they hadn't come back.

There was a church of mopane and mud with a mopane flagpole to fly a white flag when somebody died; the funeral service was more or less the same protestant one the missionaries brought from Scotland and it was combined with older rituals to entrust the newly-dead to the ancestors. Ululating women with whitened faces sent them on their way to the missionaries' last judgment. The children were baptized with names chosen by portent in consultation between the mother and an old man who read immutable fate in the fall of small bones cast like dice from a horn cup. On all occasions and most Saturday nights there was a beer-drink, which the chief attended. An upright chair from his house was brought out for him although everyone else squatted comfortably on the sand, and he was offered the first taste from an old decorated gourd dipper (other people drank from baked-bean or pilchard tins) – it is the way of people of the village.

It is also the way of the tribe to which the clan belongs and the subcontinent to which the tribe belongs, from Matadi in the west to Mombasa in the east, from Entebbe in the north to Empangeni in the south, that everyone is welcome at a beer-drink. No traveller or passer-by, poling down the river in his pirogue, leaving the snake-skin trail of his bicycle wheels through the sand, betraying his approach – if the dogs are sleeping by the cooking fires and the children have left their home-made highways – only by the brittle fragmentation of the dead leaves as he comes unseen through miles of mopane, is a presence to be questioned. Everyone for a long way round on both sides of the border near Dilolo has a black skin, speaks the same language and shares the custom of hospitality. Before the government started to shoot people at night to stop more young men leaving when no one was awake to ask, 'Where are you going?' people thought nothing of walking ten miles from one village to another for a beer-drink.

But unfamiliar faces have become unusual. If the firelight caught such a face, it backed into darkness. No one remarked the face. Not even the smallest child who never took its eyes off it, crouching down among the knees of men with soft, little boy's lips held in wonderingly over teeth as if an invisible grown-up hand were clamped there. The young girls giggled and flirted from the background, as usual. The older men didn't ask for news of relatives or friends outside the village. The chief seemed not to see one face or faces in distinction from any other. His eyes came to rest instead on some of the older men. He gazed and they felt it.

Coming out of the back door of his brick house with its polished concrete steps, early in the morning, he hailed one of them. The man was passing with his hobbling cows and steadily bleating goats; stopped, with the turn of one who will continue on his way in a moment almost without breaking step. But the summons was for him. The chief wore a frayed collarless shirt and old trousers, like the man, but he was never barefoot. In the hand with a big steel watch on the wrist, he carried his thick-framed spectacles, and drew down his nose between the fingers of the other hand; he had the authoritative body of a man who still has his sexual powers but his eyes flickered against the light of the sun and secreted flecks of matter like cold cream at the corners. After the greetings usual between a chief and one of his headmen together with whom, from the retreat in the mopane forest where they lay together in the same age-group recovering from circumcision, he had long ago emerged a man, the chief said, 'When is your son coming back?'

'I have no news.'

'Did he sign for the mines?'

'No.'

'He's gone to the tobacco farms?'

'He didn't tell us.'

'Gone away to find work and doesn't tell his mother? What sort of child is that? Didn't you teach him?'

The goats were tongue-ing three hunchback bushes that were all that was left of a hedge round the chief's house. The man took out a round tin dented with child's tooth-marks and taking care not to spill any snuff, dosed himself. He gestured at the beasts, for permission: 'They're eating up your house . . .' He made a move towards the necessity to drive them on.

'There is nothing left there to eat.' The chief ignored his hedge, planted by his oldest wife who had been to school at the mission up the river. He stood among the goats as if he would ask more questions. Then he turned and went back to his yard, dismissing himself. The other man watched. It seemed he might call after; but instead drove his animals with the familiar cries, this time unnecessarily loud and frequent.

Often an army patrol Land Rover came to the village. No one could predict when this would be because it was not possible to count the days in between and be sure that so many would elapse before it returned, as could be done in the case of a tax-collector or cattle-dipping officer. But it could be heard minutes away, crashing through the mopane like a frightened animal, and dust hung marking the direction from which it was coming. The children ran to tell. The women went from hut to hut. One of the chief's wives would enjoy the importance of bearing the news: 'The government is coming to see you.' He would be out of his house when the Land Rover stopped and a black soldier (murmuring towards the chief the required respectful greeting in their own language) jumped out and opened the door for the white soldier. The white soldier had learned the names of all the local chiefs. He gave greetings with white men's brusqueness: 'Everything all right?' And the chief repeated to him: 'Everything all right.' 'No one been bothering you in this village?' 'No one is troubling us.' But the white soldier signalled to his black men and they went through every hut busy as wives when they are cleaning, turning over bedding, thrusting gun-butts into the pile of ash and rubbish where the chickens searched, even looking in, their eyes dazzled by darkness, to the hut where one of the old women who had gone crazy had to be kept most of the time. The white soldier stood beside the Land Rover waiting for them. He told the chief of things that were happening not far from the village; not far at all. The road that passed five kilometres away had been blown up. 'Someone plants land-mines in the road and as soon as we repair it they put them there again. Those people come from across the river and they pass this way. They wreck our vehicles and kill people.'

The heads gathered round weaved as if at the sight of bodies laid there horrifyingly before them.

'They will kill you, too – burn your huts, all of you – if you let them stay with you.'

A woman turned her face away: 'Aïe-aïe-aïe-aïe.'

His forefinger half-circled his audience. 'I'm telling you. You'll see what they do.'

The chief's latest wife, taken only the year before and of the age-group of his elder grandchildren, had not come out to listen to the white man. But she heard from others what he had said, and fiercely smoothing her legs with grease, demanded of the chief, 'Why does he want us to die, that white man!'

Her husband, who had just been a passionately shuddering lover, became at once one of the important old with whom she did not count and could not argue. 'You talk about things you don't know. Don't speak for the sake of making a noise.'

To punish him, she picked up the strong, young girl's baby she had borne him and went out of the room where she slept with him on the big bed that had come down the river by barge, before the army's machine guns were pointing at the other bank.

He appeared at his mother's hut. There, the middle-aged man on whom the villagers depended, to whom the government looked when it wanted taxes paid and culling orders carried out, became a son – the ageless category, no matter from which age-group to another he passed in the progression of her life and his. The old woman was at her toilet. The great weight of her body settled around her where she sat on a reed mat outside the door. He pushed a stool under himself. Set out was a small mirror with a pink plastic frame and stand, in which he caught sight of his face, screwed up. A large black comb; a little carved box inlaid with red lucky beans she had always had, he used to beg to be allowed to play with it fifty years ago. He waited, not so much out of respect as in the bond of indifference to all outside their mutual contact that reasserts itself when lions and their kin lie against one another.

She cocked a glance, swinging the empty loops of her stretched ear-lobes. He did not say what he had come for.

She had chosen a tiny bone spoon from the box and was poking with trembling care up each round hole of distended nostril. She cleaned the crust of dried snot and dust from her delicate instrument and flicked the dirt in the direction away from him.

She said: 'Do you know where your sons are?'

'Yes, I know where my sons are. You have seen three of them here today. Two are in school at the mission. The baby – he's with the mother.' A slight smile, to which the old woman did not respond. Her preferences among the sons had no connection with sexual pride.

'Good. You can be glad of all that. But don't ask other people about theirs.'

As often when people who share the same blood share the same thought, for a moment mother and son looked exactly alike, he old-womanish, she mannish.

'If the ones we know are missing, there are not always empty places,' he said.

She stirred consideringly in her bulk. Leaned back to regard him: 'It used to be that all children were our own children. All sons our sons. *Old-fashion*, these people here' – the hard English word rolled out of their language like a pebble, and came to rest where aimed, at his feet.

It was spring: the mopane leaves turn, drying up and dying, spattering the sand with blood and rust – a battlefield, it must have looked, from the patrol planes. In August there is no rain to come for two months yet. Nothing grows but the flies hatch. The heat rises daily and the nights hold it, without a stir, till morning. On these nights the radio voice carried so clearly it could be heard from the chief's house all through the village. Many were being captured in the bush and killed by the army – *seek and destroy* was what the white men said now – and many in the army were being set upon in the bush or blown up in their trucks and buried with full military honours. This was expected to continue until October because the men in the bush knew that it was their last chance before the rains came and chained their feet in mud.

On these hot nights when people cannot sleep anyway, beer-drinks last until very late. People drink more; the women know this, and brew more. There is a fire but no one sits close round it.

Without a moon the dark is thick with heat; when the moon is full the dark shimmers thinly in a hot mirage off the river. Black faces are blue, there are watermarks along noses and biceps. The chief sat on his chair and wore shoes and socks in spite of the heat; those drinking nearest him could smell the suffering of his feet. The planes of jaw and lips he noticed in moonlight molten over them, moonlight pouring moths broken from white cases on the mopane and mosquitoes rising from the river, pouring glory like the light in the religious pictures people got at the mission – he had seen those faces about lately in the audacity of day, as well. An ox had been killed and there was the scent of meat sizzling in the village (just look at the behaviour of the dogs, they knew) although there was no marriage or other festival that called for someone to slaughter one of his beasts. When the chief allowed himself, at least, to meet the eyes of a stranger, the whites that had been showing at an oblique angle disappeared and he took rather than saw the full gaze of the seeing eye: the pupils with their defiance, their belief, their claim, hold, on him. He let it happen only once. For the rest, he saw their arrogant lifted jaws to each other and warrior smiles to the girls, as they drank. The children were drawn to them, fighting one another silently for places close up. Towards midnight – his watch had its own glowing galaxy – he left his chair and did not come back from the shadows where men went to urinate. Often at beer-drinks the chief would go home while others were still drinking.

He went to his brick house whose roof shone almost bright as day. He did not go to the room where his new wife and sixth son would be sleeping in the big bed, but simply took from the kitchen, where it was kept when not in use, a bicycle belonging to one of his hangers-on, relative or retainer. He wheeled it away from the huts in the clearing, his village and grandfather's village that disappeared so quickly behind him in the mopane, and began to ride through the sand. He was not afraid he would meet a patrol and be shot; alone at night in the sand forest, the forested desert he had known before and would know beyond his span of life, he didn't believe in the power of a roving band of government men to end that life. The going was heavy but he had mastered when young the art of riding on this, the only terrain he knew, and the ability came back. In an hour he arrived at the army post, called out who he was to the sentry with a machine gun, and had to wait, like a beggar rather than a chief, to be allowed to approach and be searched. There were black soldiers on duty but they woke the white man. It was the one who knew his name, his clan, his village, the way these modern white men were taught. He seemed to know at once why the chief had come; frowning in concentration to grasp details, his mouth was open in a smile and the point of his tongue curled touching at back teeth the way a man will verify facts one by one on his fingers. 'How many?'

'Six or ten or – but sometimes it's only, say, three or one . . . I don't know. One is here, he's gone; they come again.'

'They take food, they sleep, and off. Yes. They make the

people give them what they want, that's it, eh? And you know who it is who hides them – who shows them where to sleep – of course you know.'

The chief sat on one of the chairs in that place, the army's place, and the white soldier was standing. 'Who is it –' the chief was having difficulty in saying what he wanted in English, he had the feeling it was not coming out as he had meant nor being understood as he had expected. 'I can't know who is it' – a hand moved restlessly, he held a breath and released it – 'in the village there's many, plenty people. If it's this one or this one –' He stopped, shaking his head with a reminder to the white man of his authority, which the white soldier was quick to placate. 'Of course. Never mind. They frighten the people; the people can't say no. They kill people who say no, eh; cut their ears off, you know that? Tear away their lips. Don't you see the pictures in the papers?'

'We never saw it. I heard the government say on the radio.'

'They're still drinking . . . How long – an hour ago?'

The white soldier checked with a look the other men, whose stance had changed to that of bodies ready to break into movement: grab weapons, run, fling themselves at the Land Rovers guarded in the dark outside. He picked up the telephone receiver but blocked the mouth-piece as if it were someone about to make an objection. 'Chief, I'll be with you in a moment. – Take him to the duty room and make coffee. Just wait –' he leaned his full reach towards a drawer in a cabinet on the left of the desk and, scrabbling to get it open, took out a half-full bottle of brandy. Behind the chief's back he gestured the bottle towards the chief, and a black soldier jumped obediently to take it.

The chief went to a cousin's house in a village the other side of the army post later that night. He said he had been to a beer-drink and could not ride home because of the white men's curfew.

The white soldier had instructed that he should not be in his own village when the arrests were made so that he could not be connected with these and would not be in danger of having his ears cut off for taking heed of what the government wanted of him, or having his lips mutilated for what he had told.

His cousin gave him blankets. He slept in a hut with her father. The deaf old man was aware neither that he had come nor was leaving so early that last night's moon, the size of the bicycle's reflector, was still shiny in the sky. The bicycle rode up on spring-hares without disturbing them, in the forest; there was a stink of jackal-fouling still sharp on the dew. Smoke already marked his village; early cooking fires were lit. Then he saw that the smoke, the black particles spindling at his face, were not from cooking fires. Instead of going faster as he pumped his feet against the weight of sand the bicycle seemed to slow along with his mind, to find in each revolution of its wheels the countersurge: to stop; not go on. But there was no way not to reach what he found. The planes only children bothered to look up at any longer had come in the night and dropped something terrible and alive that no one could have read or heard about enough to be sufficiently afraid of. He saw first a bloody kaross, a dog caught on the roots of an upturned tree. The earth under the village seemed to have burst open and flung away what it carried: the huts, pots, gourds, blankets, the tin trunks, alarm-clocks, curtain-booth photographs, bicycles, radios and shoes brought back from the mines, the bright cloths young wives wound on their heads, the pretty pictures of white lambs and pink children at the knees of the golden-haired Christ the Scottish Mission Board first brought long ago – all five generations of the clan's life that had been chronicled by each succeeding generation in episodes told to the next. The huts had staved in like broken anthills. Within earth walls baked and streaked by fire the thatch and roof-poles were ash. He bellowed and stumbled from hut to hut, nothing answered frenzy, not even a chicken rose from under his feet. The walls of his house still stood. It was gutted and the roof had buckled. A black stiff creature lay roasted on its chain in the yard. In one of the huts he saw a human shape transformed the same way, a thing of stiff tar daubed on a recognizable framework. It was the hut where the mad woman lived; when those who had survived fled, they had forgotten her.

The chief's mother and his youngest wife were not among them. But the baby boy lived, and will grow up in the care of the older wives. No one can say what it was the white soldier said over the telephone to his commanding officer, and if the commanding officer had told him what was going to be done, or whether the white soldier knew, as a matter of procedure laid down in his military training for this kind of war, what would be done. The chief hanged himself in the mopane. The police or the army (much the same these days, people confuse them) found the bicycle beneath his dangling shoes. So the family hanger-on still rides it; it would have been lost if it had been safe in the kitchen when the raid came. No one knows where the chief found a rope, in the ruins of his village.

The people are beginning to go back. The dead are properly buried in ancestral places in the mopane forest. The women are to be seen carrying tins and grain panniers of mud up from the river. In talkative bands they squat and smear, raising the huts again. They bring sheaves of reeds exceeding their own height, balanced like the cross-stroke of a majuscular T on their heads. The men's voices sound through the mopane as they choose and fell trees for the roof supports.

A white flag on a mopane pole hangs outside the house whose white walls, built like a white man's, stand from before this time.

MORE ABOUT PENGUINS, PELICANS AND PUFFINS

Nadine Gordimer in Penguin

A WORLD OF STRANGERS

Toby Hood, a young Englishman, shuns the politics and the causes his liberal parents passionately support. Living in Johannesburg as a representative of his family's publishing company, Toby moves easily, carelessly, between the complacent wealthy white suburbs and the seething, vibrantly alive black townships. His friends include a wide variety of people, from mining directors to black journalists and musicians, and Toby's colonial-style weekends are often interspersed with clandestine evenings spent in black shanty towns.

Toby's friendship with Steven Sithole, a dashing, embittered young African, touches him in ways he never thought possible, and when Steven's own sense of independence from the rules of society leads to tragedy, Toby's life is changed forever.

'[Gordimer's] characters are universal. It is to the moments of greatest stress, when frail structures of idealism are being tested by shaking realities, that Miss Gordimer gives the form of literature' – *The New York Times*

'A triumphant success' – *Observer*

Nadine Gordimer in Penguin

THE LATE BOURGEOIS WORLD

'Superb . . . [Nadine] Gordimer's persuasiveness is achieved with one of the lightest and yet most inexorable touches you will find in contemporary writing' – *The New York Times*

Liz Van Den Sandt's ex-husband, Max, an ineffectual rebel, has drowned himself. In prison for a failed act of violence against the government, he had betrayed his colleagues.

Now Liz has been asked to perform a direct service for the black nationalist movement, at considerable danger to herself. Can she take such a risk in the face of Max's example of the uselessness of such actions? Yet . . . how can she not?

'Miss Gordimer has earned herself a place among the few novelists who really matter' – *Observer*

Nadine Gordimer in Penguin

A GUEST OF HONOUR

'A novel of total immersions – physical, moral, social, political. It teems with human life, with landscapes of the map and of the mind, with events and insights' – *Guardian*

James Bray, an English colonial administrator who was expelled from a central African nation for siding with its black nationalist leaders, is invited back ten years later to join in the country's independence celebrations. As he witnesses the factionalism and violence that erupt as revolutionary ideals are subverted by ambition and greed, Bray is once again forced to choose sides, a choice that becomes both his triumph and his undoing.

Nadine Gordimer in Penguin

LIVINGSTONE'S COMPANIONS

In these sixteen stories Nadine Gordimer deftly evokes the Africa of today, where, up-country and in town, Livingstone's 'fatal impact' still reverberates.

'Nadine Gordimer's stories are poised over the dilemmas of Africa and its denizens of both shades . . . she is always more interested in people, and what makes them happy and unhappy, than in political moralities' – *Spectator*

'Its originality is timeless and to me this is her best work: her incomparably precise, witty, unwhiny observations are webbed here with genius' – *New Statesman*

Nadine Gordimer in Penguin

THE CONSERVATIONIST

'A triumph of style . . . this is a novel of enormous power' – Paul Theroux in the *New Statesman*

Mehring is rich. He has all that white privilege in South Africa can give him. Isolated, at once cold and passionate, he challenges history in his determination that nothing shall change his way of life.

But Africa cannot be bought by the white man, now.

'One of those rare works of literature that command special respect reserved for artistic daring and fulfilled ambition' – Paul Bailey in the *Observer*

'The sounds, smells and foliage, the weaving lights of the veld, are evoked in the passages of cool delicate prose that prove their author one of the ablest descriptive writers alive' – Peter Kerr-Jarrett in the *Sunday Telegraph*

Nadine Gordimer in Penguin

BURGER'S DAUGHTER

In this brilliantly realized work Nadine Gordimer unfolds the story of a young woman's slowly evolving identity in the turbulent political environment of present-day South Africa. The prison death of her father, Lionel, leaves Rosa Burger alone to explore the intricacies of what it really means to be Burger's daughter. Moving through sensuously described landscapes in Europe and South Africa, through painful love affairs and an overwhelming flood of memories that will not release her, she arrives at last at an understanding of a life bounded on all sides by forces not of her own choosing. Nadine Gordimer's subtle, fastidiously crafted prose sweeps this engrossing narrative to a tragic and triumphant conclusion.

'A riveting history of South Africa and a penetrating portrait of a courageous woman' – *New Yorker*

Nadine Gordimer in Penguin

A SOLDIER'S EMBRACE

'Nadine Gordimer is one of the finest practitioners of the short-story form' – *Chicago Tribune*

When Nadine Gordimer's *Selected Stories* was published in 1976, Graham Greene called it 'a magnificent collection worthy of all homage'. *A Soldier's Embrace* demonstrates once more that Gordimer is one of the most accomplished writers now working in English, 'extraordinary not only for her style but also for her moral concern'. In this masterful new group of stories she continues to explore the emotional and physical landscapes of South Africa, through powerful themes that know no geographic boundaries.

'Nadine Gordimer tells us of the strange and immensely moving peril of being a woman in South Africa, as well as the strange and immensely moving peril of the races' – *The New York Review of Books*

'Like the great nineteenth-century novelists she unites vast scope with minute attention to the ordinary. Gordimer's setting is Africa . . . but in her Africa we find ourselves' – *Washington Post*

Nadine Gordimer in Penguin

JULY'S PEOPLE

It is war. For years the situation has been 'deteriorating'. Now all over South Africa the cities are battlegrounds, Bam and Maureen Smales – enlightened, liberal whites – are rescued from the terror by their servant, July, who leads them to refuge in his native village.

What happens to the Smales, and to July, mirrors the changes in the world – and gives us glimpses into a chasm of hatred and misunderstanding.

'A brave and imaginative book and should be read' – *Listener*

'Every sentence she writes has the special impress of a true novelist's imagination' – *Sunday Times*

'Adventurous, powerful and despairing' – *Financial Times*

'It is so flawlessly written that every one of its events seems chillingly, ominously possible' – *The New York Times Book Review*

Nadine Gordimer in Penguin

SOMETHING OUT THERE

This powerful collection of short stories and a novella reflects Nadine Gordimer's extraordinary ability to illuminate the connexion between the personal and the political in the divided society of South Africa. With compassion and scrupulous honesty Gordimer penetrates to the core of the human heart, revealing the subtlest feelings of her characters – black and white, revolutionaries and racists, adulterers, spinsters and lovers.

The long novella that is the centrepiece of this book is the story of a white couple and two black revolutionaries counterpointed with reports of a strange creature ravaging an elite suburb of Johannesburg. As she depicts these ironically parallel situations, Gordimer conveys the tremors of a violent universe beyond the specific events. And she brilliantly captures here, and in the other stories, the inner tremors caused by love, despair, betrayal and exultation.

'One of the major artistic achievements of our time' – Elizabeth Hardwick in *The New York Review of Books*

'Outstanding . . . it is in the conviction which Nadine Gordimer brings to her wise understanding of human relationships that she luminously excels' – *The Times*

Also published:

SELECTED STORIES

'A magnificent collection worthy of all homage' – Graham Greene

Containing stories selected from *The Soft Voice of the Serpent*, *Six Feet of the Country*, *Friday's Footprint*, *Not for Publication* and *Livingstone's Companions*.